Josh,
What var.
make jobs

Stones in my Passway

a novel of devils, deals and modern manhood

Jim Jackson

kouros
PUBLICATIONS

kouros publications

ISBN 978-0-9953259-2-0

For every man who didn't just walk away.
And for some who did.

Track Listing

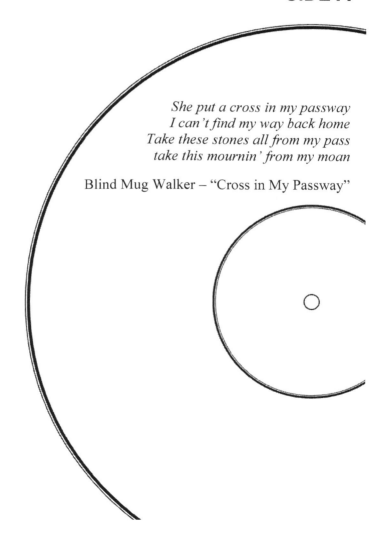

She put a cross in my passway
I can't find my way back home
Take these stones all from my pass
take this mournin' from my moan

Blind Mug Walker – "Cross in My Passway"

1. LAST FAIR DEAL GONE DOWN

When the devil came to me at a lonely crossroads in the December pre-dawn and offered me a deal, I shouldn't have listened to that damn tickle in the back of my brain that shouted *jump*.

But I had an opportunity to make an alteration to my life story. I took it. Maybe others would have had more resolve. Maybe others would have realized that what they're searching for has been in their own backyard all along. Maybe others had more motivational posters on their walls. But I thought I'd made a mistake way back before I knew that some mistakes were irreversible. I thought I'd missed the life I was supposed to lead, only by a few degrees, but now, fifteen years later, those few degrees led to an ocean-wide gulf separating me from where I was supposed to be. Laura called it not following my bliss and would recommend a chakra alignment. If that's a thing. She'd recommend some kind of woo-woo spiritual thing. Basically, my blessings had come to feel commonplace.

The cold wind cut razor tracks into my cheeks as I knelt at the crossroads of the disused railway line that crossed secondary highway 432.

I turned around knowing he was there before I heard his heels crunch on the gravel. He was almost invisible in the blackness. His dark skin and his charcoal suit eased and blurred into the night. All I could see clearly was the crisp white of his shirt and the gleam of his grin. His old-fashioned felt trilby was perched at a precarious angle and looked about ready to fall.

There was something about his eyes. Something calculating and yellow. Something mischievous and ancient. Something that suggested sickness and flies swarming around swollen bellies. The glint in his eyes made me more uneasy than being interrupted in the sureness of solitude in the wee small hours on the outskirts of town at the crossroads.

But, as he came closer, it wasn't his old-fashioned clothes or the yellowed eyes that struck me strangest. It was his hands. The fingers were long and stretched, with knobbly knuckles punctuating them at inhuman intervals. They were fingers like the legs of some deep-sea creature. They were alien autopsy fingers, and he waved them in front of his face as he walked toward me.

"Hiya, pal. Don't get up, don't get up," he said still grinning. "I'm not fixing to disturb you, my man. Just wanted to see if you'll be needing any help on this here wicked-cold night. What can Papa Scratch do you for?"

I was still semi-crouched, my hand on the gravel where I'd buried what I thought was a human finger bone with cuneiform carvings that I'd gotten from a mystical, homeless guy earlier that night. I straightened up slowly. I looked to his trim mustache under his broad flat nose so I wouldn't have to look into his yellowed eyes.

"I – I was just … I'm not sure what I was doing," I said and pulled on my beard. When I was a seven, my mother caught me playing with my sister's Barbie dolls. Nothing wrong with that, of course – it's not like I was putting them into weird sex positions or anything – but having an adult burst in like that made me feel like I'd committed some sin against nature. I felt like that again as he walked up to me.

Papa Scratch twirled a toothpick around in his grinning teeth. "No need to explain, man. I gotcha, I gotcha. I dig, man. I really do." He took a step closer and clicked his teeth together three times. "You want to make a deal."

I said nothing.

"Hold on a tick, pal o' mine," he said and turned around. "I just gotta deal with something."

From the copse of trees behind him, I heard what sounded like a baby bawl. I squinted and saw a flash of white fur bouncing and leaping in random patterns. It bleated again.

Papa Scratch pinched the bridge of his nose with his long fingers. "What the heck I's supposed to do with a *goat*?" He turned to me. "I mean *seriously*. Some cult in Middelfart, Denmark wants to worship me – and don't get me wrong, I'm lovin' the sentiment. But the execution. I mean, *come on* – a pygmy goat? I ain't been into goats since I left the ziggurat."

I tried to nod sympathetically.

He looked back to the goat and shrugged. "Still, a meal's a meal."

In a motion, he scooped up the bleating thing and stretched his jaw so his chin rested halfway down his belly.

Wait – what? Meal?

"No!" I called out instinctively. I lurched forward, caught my toe on the railway track and fell sprawlingly into Papa Scratch, knocking the goat from his hands.

My eyes shot to him. His jaw still hung open wide as we both watched the little white thing prance into the field behind the tracks. Neither of us said anything. I looked up at him, and he gaped down at me.

He spoke first, retracting his jaw to more human proportions. "Well, heck. Goats ain't really my thing, anyway, man," he said and waggled his long fingers.

I breathed again. And wished I'd given the animal some of Laura's granola from my pocket.

He shot a withering look at me. "But don't be thinking you're off the hook, pal o' mine. You owe me one. Maybe even *two*."

"Oh, do I?" I said and raised an eyebrow. "And what would happen if I just walked away?"

He smiled, and his teeth looked luminescent in the pre-dawn. "If you walk away, my boys and me will swallow your eternal soul while it screams."

I should have laughed it off, but something in the way he said it reminded me of a nightmare I'd had once where I was the devil himself, casting souls into hell, and I shivered. Okay. I'd play along and see where this went. "Fine. I owe you one. But I'm afraid I'm fresh out of goats. I think I have some kielbasas in the freezer – would that do?"

"Aw, Wood, my man."

Had I mentioned my name?

"It'll take more than meat in tube form to make it up to me." He steepled his long fingers and clicked his teeth together again repeatedly. "I want to know *why*."

"Why I have kielbasas in the freezer?" I forced a smile.

He grunted. "Why here? Why that?" He gestured to spot where I'd buried the carved bone.

Okay. I wanted to see where this went now. "Fine," I said. "You want my story? It started with a phone call. I should have been asleep when the police called."

If I'd just been asleep at a reasonable hour for a forty-year-old on that Sunday night two days before Christmas Eve – if I'd just let Laura answer the phone and deal with things by saying everyone involved was just following the holy contour of the universe – maybe I never would have been out here on these crossroads or met the little man who called himself Papa Scratch.

That phone call still bounced around my lack-of-sleep-addled brain as I stared into the yellow eyes of the little man in the old-fashioned suit.

I should have been asleep.

"Mr. Wood Sweeney?" the woman's voice on the other end said in even, practiced tones.

"Yes. What? Yes. Yes, that's me."

"This is Constable Santiago. You have a daughter – Miss Makayla Sweeney?"

I had a sinking feeling, and my mouth turned sticky. Through the red panic I saw my daughter, just a few hours old, and her mother asleep in the hospital bed, still a little miffed she wasn't allowed to burn incense in the delivery room. I held Makayla in the wickedly uncomfortable hospital chair as dawn broke on the first day of her life.

She was warm on my shoulder, and I expected her to be so much heavier.

"Yes." My voice cracked as I snapped back to reality. I didn't try to cover it up by clearing my throat. "Is she alright?"

"She's fine. She's with us. We found her at the River Landing in possession of open bottles of beer."

My blood started moving again. She's not dead. Everything else we can deal with. Wait, what did she say? "Bottles? Plural? How many did she have?" Whoops. Was that too flippant?

"She had two open bottles, sir. And two unopened ones. She was with a friend. They each had one open bottle of beer." There was a pause. "Would it be alright if I gave her a ride home and talked to you for a moment?"

Yep. Too flippant.

"Um, it might actually be just as easy if I came to pick her up. I don't want to trouble you. You're still at the river, are you?"

"It's no trouble, sir." There was another pause. I had an urge to say something, but I knew anything that came out of my mouth now would sound incriminating. Everything that came out of my mouth usually sounded incriminating, even I wasn't talking to the police. The pause got longer. "It's no trouble at all, sir." There was another, even longer pause. "Makayla gave your address as six-one-six Eastlake Avenue. Is that correct?"

I told her it was.

"We'll see you shortly, then."

That could have played out better. I wish I'd just insisted on picking her up. But Constable what's-her-name probably wanted to size me up and see if I was the one who drove Mak to drinking. Like she was some kind of saint.

I screwed the top back on my bottle of Ballantine's.

Right. I could handle this myself. No need to wake Laura up. I'd break it to her gently tomorrow morning. Or get Mak to. Now the trick was just to keep everything nice and calm and cool and quiet.

When the car pulled up, I was waiting at the door. No doorbells, no knocking. Mak bowed her head when the officer let her out of the back door of the cop car, but came slowly up the walk with her chin held high.

Officer Saintly ducked as she came through the door. Outside, hands on his hips, and probably as broad in the shoulders as he was tall, was what I assumed was her partner. He was the *bad cop* of the two, if police actually did things like that in real life. He stared at the scene and said nothing, only occasionally taking hands from hips to lift his hat and run his palm across the blonde stubble on his head.

Officer Saintly stepped inside after Mak. "How have things been at home, Mr. Sweeney? Have you or your wife had any disagreements with Makayla recently?"

I took the insinuation on the chin. The acid bubbled up in my gut, but I played along to see where this went.

"No, ma'am." I said in calm, cool, collected tones. "Nothing more than the usual power struggles." I lied. Laura and Mak constantly tossed back and forth those little, barbed attacks that seem perfectly innocuous unless you know they're not supposed to be – Laura trying to take the high road by saying *she* wasn't disappointed in Mak, but that this wasn't the path the *universe* had in store for her. I felt the acid rise in my gut at the thought. Mak would just roll her eyes. But she was a good kid. How could I get across to Officer Saintly that my daughter was far more likely to be caught frantically trying to capture a changing light in her sketchbook than drinking cheap beer by the river? And her sketches were pretty good. I'd peeked at some of them – I guess the devil made me do it. She was probably better than I would have been, even if I hadn't given it all up when Laura got pregnant.

I looked at Mak. She didn't have her sketchbook.

"Makayla," Officer Saintly said, softening her tone even more. "How are things at home?"

Mak shrugged. Officer Saintly didn't say anything for a long time. She knew if she made the pause long enough, someone would fill it. Don't cave to the silence, Mak.

"They don't understand me," Makayla said finally.

"Who doesn't understand you? Your parents?"

Mak shrugged again, her eyes cast down, but then pre-empted the constable's next inevitable silence. "No one. I see things. At school."

"Look," I said, in tones not as calm, cool and collected as I would have liked. "This is just kids' stuff. *Nobody understands me*. I went through it." I looked up at Officer Saintly. "You, I'm sure, went through it. Let me just deal with this drinking thing, and we can call it a night." My confidence in myself as a father wobbled.

"What do you mean by *deal with*, sir?"

"What? I mean I'll talk to her. Like parents do. I didn't mean I was going to hit her or anything."

Officer Saintly took half a step back and Partner tensed his shoulders. "What makes you bring up violence? Makayla, do you feel safe spending the night in this house? We can make other arrangements."

"Jesus fuck! She's fine here. We're all fine. There's nothing to worry about." I put my arm around Makayla's shoulder. She shrugged it off and pulled away. Great. The little girl who'd do anything for her dad – who'd offer to give up seven weeks of her allowance to buy me a new straw hat to replace the one she'd crushed playing astronaut dress-up – was gone.

"Sir, there's no need to raise your voice. Maybe we should talk to Mrs. Sweeney?"

There certainly *was* a reason to raise my voice. But, no. Calm, cool and collected, right? "No need for that. Really"

"No *need* for that?" Laura said from behind me. "You weren't going to tell me about this?"

I spun around. "Of course I was. Tomorrow. I knew if you came down now you'd just –"

I caught myself. I didn't know exactly what I was going to say, but I knew it wouldn't have ended well.

"I'd just what? Show our daughter that there are consequences for her actions? That you can't harm yourself without harming the sacred order of things? Yeah. Yeah, I would have. I will. I'm not going to just laugh it off as a rite of passage or something. She's committed an offense against the best parts of herself."

Officer Saintly stepped toward Laura. "Mrs. Sweeney, I'd like to talk to you and Makayla in private for a moment. Mr. Sweeney? Could you please step outside?"

"Step outside of my own house? What – while you ask my family if they feel safe with me or something?"

She said nothing. Again. This time I broke the silence and cursed myself for it.

"Fine." I turned and went outside, pulling the door clanglingly shut behind me. Flippancy *and* petulance in the face of the law – is that what my four decades on this planet taught me?

I shivered. I realized that I was in my pyjamas and shifted from foot to foot. Partner didn't move. I'm not even sure I saw him blink. I nodded at him in the kind of basic, humanity-affirming yet curt nod that you'd give passing someone in the men's room. He lifted his hat and rubbed his hand across his head stubble. My confidence as a father guttered.

It wasn't the first time I'd been out in the cold with the police. The afternoon before Colin Ackerman's exhibition – he was a photographer who liked to pass off his porn pics as *The Nude as Landscape* – he wailed on his girlfriend in a fit of nerves, leaving her bruised and bloody. I called the cops. They took her statement and told her domestic abuse cases are hard to prove. They asked her what she did to provoke him. And I did nothing. I felt the same acid rise in my gut.

It was later that night that Laura told me she was pregnant. I told her I'd stay with her. Laura believed wholeheartedly that the universe wanted us to be together – she'd told me that on our fourth date. Who was I to argue with the universe? I told her we'd see where it went. Turns out it went to me being in my pyjamas on the frozen lawn while the police questioned my family. About me.

The door opened, and Officer Saintly gave Partner a look. He nodded and went to the car.

"Thank you for your patience," Officer Saintly said to me, silhouetted by the light from inside the house. "We need to be thorough in this kind of situation. You understand." She came down the two steps from the house to where I was standing and held out an awkward hand. "She's a good kid. Help her make the right decisions." We shook hands for slightly longer than I thought was normal, but I was happy for the warmth. "She has my number. But I don't want to see any of you again. Understand?"

"Yes, officer," I said, feeling like I'd been the one caught with cheap beer in public. I even said *thanks*.

Laura was already laying into Makayla when I got inside. "How could you do something like this? How could you do something like this to *yourself*? Don't you have any self-respect? Drinking – it's just so mundane. I understand you want to establish a sense of your own identity, but this is a really dull way to do it. And just before *Christmas*."

The acid rose again in my gut. "Laura, go easy on her." I regretted it as soon as I said it. "Tell you what – why don't we all get away? Forget Christmas this year. We could jet off to someplace sunny and tourist-drenched, wear botanical print shirts and cameras around our necks? Hell, maybe we'll even move there. I'll build a house by the beach –"

"*You'll* build a house?" Laura asked.

"Well, I'll get some help building a house by the beach, I'll paint, Mak'll draw, you'll garden – think of what you could grow! – and we'll kick the slump this family has been in for the last few years. Come on – go pack a bikini." That sounded sufficiently dad-like to bring my fatherly confidence up a couple notches.

Laura's solid rock face broke suddenly into a smile. "What about Christmas dinner with my parents?"

I cocked an eyebrow and pulled on my beard in mock-contemplation. "Hm. I guess two birds, then. We get to spend some time together *and* miss out on dinner with your parents. I'll go book the tickets."

"Mak?" I said, turning to her. "What's your vote? Hawaii? Mexico? Pitcairn Islands? Some undiscovered paradise where the locals are so grateful to have visitors they wait on us hand and foot in appropriate-yet-somewhat-revealing traditional garb?"

She was quiet. Her eyes were on the floor. She was never quiet.

"I'm not going on vacation." I could barely hear her.

"What?" Laura and I said at the same time.

Makayla looked up, her cheeks stained with tears, but her eyes dry now. "I'm not going on vacation."

"Excuse me young lady," Laura started. "Your father might use humor at ridiculously inappropriate times, but you could at least go along –"

"I'm not going on fucking *vacation*! There are kids dying – *dying* – at school. Josie Dilullo died on Saturday at a party. She's *dead*. She sits – sat – literally right beside me in school. She won't sit there when we go back in January. She was alive, and then she took fentanyl – she didn't even know what it *was* – and now she's dead." I watched Makayla crumble against the primal humanity of death. Her upper lip stretched tight around her teeth and the corners of her mouth pulled down in a contorted mask of tragedy. "There are kids *dying*. They all died meaninglessly. We all do. The news is calling it a pandemic."

"The news doesn't –" I attempted. Wrong move.

"I've *seen* it, Dad," she talked over me. "It gets everyone. I'm going to die meaninglessly – and you give a damn that I drank a *beer?!*" The tears came after a wail of anguish, like sheets of rain after the first thunderclap.

Laura moved in to comfort her, but Mak shrugged her off. Makayla looked up at me through the tears, challenging me to make it better. To fix it like I had so many of her toys. Dada fix.

I had nothing.

And then she was gone into the night and the cold, the screen door clanging behind her. My fatherly confidence burned, smoldered and blinked out of existence.

"I'm calling the police." The frantic was showing through Laura's tone. I wasn't going to let the same happen to me.

I forced down the panic at the thought that my daughter had weekly brushes with death because of this fentanyl crisis. I forced down my rage at the thought that it could have easily been her dead of an overdose. They mingled with the acid rising in my gut.

I focused on Officer Saintly and Partner coming back. I thought about Mak needing to spend the night, maybe several nights, somewhere – where do they even put kids? in an orphanage? I thought about court dates and social worker visits and family counseling.

And I focused on my marriage. It had always been in the shotgun family of weddings – Laura was seven months pregnant by that time. So I got a wife for my twenty-sixth birthday and kid right after that. I refused to be a divorce statistic like my parents or like Laura's parents. But I knew the threadbare remains of our marriage couldn't take the consequences of having the police come to the house twice in one night, even with Laura's steadfast belief that the universe itself wanted us to stay together. I needed us to see it through without cosmic intervention. I'd never been an adult without Laura around. I'd never had to be on my own, even when we were skirmishing along the borders of our separate selves.

"No, I'll go look for her." I said. I sounded in control. I was saying that I would go look for her, *and I would find her*.

I threw on a puffer jacket over my pyjamas, and Laura surprised me by kissing me on the cheek. "I didn't know," she whispered.

"About Josie Dilullo? I saw something on the news. I wondered if Mak knew her …"

"I understand. How do you even bring something like that up with her?"

"Yeah." There was nothing more to say. "I should go."

"Wood?"

I turned around. Laura fumbled for a plastic bag in her purse and gave it me. "Granola. In case you're out there a while."

I gave a half smile. "Thanks." I turned to go.

"Oh, and Wood?"

I turned back and raised an eyebrow.

"Nothing," she said and bowed her head. I walked out into the cold.

2. DRUNKEN HEARTED MAN

The damp settled into my bones, but I barely noticed it. I figured I'd go back to the river. I pictured myself finding Mak right away, we'd have some kind of tearful reconciliation, I'd say something wise and fatherly and that would be that. Dada fix.

A jingling sound made me turn around, and I saw a man in a dirty ski jacket and what looked like at least two pairs of pants pushing a shopping cart full of empty bottles.

"Are you lost?" he said in the even tones of someone asking the time on a busy street. Not what I expected from the only other living soul at three o'clock in the morning two days before Christmas.

I raised an eyebrow. "Me? No. No, not me. No."

"You look lost." A razor wind separated a section of his long hair and it flapped uncertainly.

Something about his manner – or the feather hanging from his shopping cart, or his long hair pulled back, smooth and clean – made me think he saw more than he was letting on. Had I met him before? This whole scene seemed *déjà vu* familiar.

"It's actually my daughter who's lost." I said, somehow comfortable spilling my story to the guy.

"No, you're lost," he said again plainly. "We have a saying," he continued, ruffling through the assorted bags and boxes in his cart, jangling the bottles. He looked in my direction but closed his eyes. "The tribe must walk before we can talk. Sweetgrass must burn before we can earn."

He opened his eyes and nodded solemnly. I said nothing, only breathed in the night air and felt ice crystals form in my nostrils.

"You understand, then?" he asked. His faced changed. He slitted his eyes, and they stared through me to the darkness of the River Landing park behind.

"I do. I do." I didn't.

"Good." He pulled out a *Victoria's Secret* bag from his shopping cart, the lingerie-clad model on its side cracked and lined from repeated stuffing in and pulling out whatever meager treasures the man kept with him. He held something out in his hand and beckoned me closer.

And I went. I should have turned away and kept looking for my daughter, but the buzzing down the back of my neck made me crunch toward him on the snow and hold out my hand. I felt like the best and oldest parts of me were resonating with this cold, turning-point night and making the world sing again, like it had when I was still painting. Like it had when Laura and I were first together.

He took me by the wrist with greasy fingers, and his hooded gaze told me, wordlessly, that I was supposed to close my eyes. I did, and something small and hard dropped into my hand. He closed my fingers around it with his.

"Thank you, Mr. ..." was all I could manage to squeeze out.

"My name's Willie Brown. In these parts."

I was sure I'd met him before. The day Colin Ackerman beat up his girlfriend. The night Laura told me she was pregnant. "I know you."

He nodded slowly.

"I was wandering out here – what? fifteen years ago? When this was still just a place that collected junk and junkies. I wanted to know what to do about the baby on the way. If I should stay." I remembered his words exactly. "You told me I had a destiny."

"You do have a destiny." Still nodding.

"Yeah – my destiny to provide for my family. You really helped me that night."

He stopped nodding. Another breeze started to blow, but died suddenly.

Then the riverside was gone. I was sitting with Willie Brown in front of a smoking fire on a vast plain. He'd changed. His long hair was pulled into two braids that draped across the skin of his dark chest. Metal discs hung from his ears, and his pants were made of what looked like coarse buffalo hide.

"You don't know why you're here, do you?" he asked. "No one told you." He looked down at the fire.

"No," was all I could say.

Willie Brown cast his eyes to the grey sky above the plain, and his face creased in pain. "There is no one left to tell them. No one who can instruct them before it's time for their trials. Just look at this one."

He turned back to me. "You're better than this, Wood."

My eyebrow shot up. "What? Thanks. But I'm not. Maybe I could have been, but I'm not."

Willie Brown turned his eyes again to the vastness of the sky. "He doesn't understand."

For less than the skin of a second, my entire field of sight was filled with fire and earth in combat, and all I could hear was the clamor of untempered struggle.

Then all was quiet on the plain. I shook my head.

On a low hill toward the horizon I saw someone. He stood, cast red by the dying light of the sky, in a battered leather jacket, Henley and jeans. He looked like me, but his face was lined in patterns of weariness that I'd never known. He smiled a humorless smile behind blank, defeated eyes, and his stance, his stare, hinted at an unveiled aggression. Toward me.

The fire cracked and shot out a spark, and my eyes instinctively followed it. When I turned back, the plain, the fire, the tent were gone. I was back in the empty park as a lonely, train-whistle sound howled, bent and dented, and full of longing and loss. A long, blue note, played on a harmonica.

I looked around for its source but saw only the dark sky and the snow-covered riverside. The stinging cold told me I was back on familiar ground again. A voice from somewhere whispered *devil slayer*.

My hand closed around whatever I was holding. I looked again at Willie Brown, now back at the helm of his bottle-filled shopping cart and wearing his grimy ski jacket.

"Take that to a sacred place. A place of crossed roads. Bury it. Your family will find peace. You may not."

"What? What do you mean I *may* not? Like, *maybe* I won't find peace, or I *can't* ever find peace?"

"I mean what I mean."

Hm. But that wasn't the real question. I wanted to ask him what question this unseen talisman in my hand was supposed to answer. The buzz of being part of something bigger than myself faded the fragile memory of that empty place dreamlike into the cold and the sharpness of what I knew to be reality. It was one of life's few perfect moments, when necessity and coincidence cross at a sacred place. It was the way I felt leaning over a table in a steamy coffee shop on my fourth date with Laura, when she told me the universe or something destined us to be together.

I opened my mouth to try to thank Willie Brown for all of this.

My phone rang instead.

Someone was on the other end, but there was no *hi*. Just the sounds of far-off talking.

"Laura? Is that you? Are you there?"

Her voice was muffled. It sounded like she was yelling at someone.

"Laura? It's me."

"Wood, are you coming home? I've been dealing with Makayla on my own here for the last hour."

What? Jesus fuck. "Makayla is there? You couldn't have told me? I've been –"

"Wood, I don't have time for this. I don't think you should come back right away. She needs a strong hand now, not someone laughing this off as a rite of passage like you would. We'll talk tomorrow. I'm going to hang up now."

I don't know how long I stood there with the phone to my ear. A wind picked up, and the scant bit of warmth I'd kindled walking dissipated into the late December night.

"No," I said aloud to no one. "No, I shouldn't come back right away. I'll let you lay in to her, then I'll come in as the good cop." A vision of myself, in full fatherly glory and using the calm, cool, collected tones of Officer Saintly, came to me. Now I just had to live up to it.

And to kill a couple of hours before going home.

I put the phone away and kept walking. But not back across the bridge home. I just walked. Out of downtown. Out of the city. At some point, I wandered onto a stretch of disused railway tracks, and the steady crunch of gravel lent a punctuation to an anger that slowly came over me as I relived the conversation again.

The acid rose in my gut.

She couldn't have told me Mak had been at home for the last hour? No. Instead she just tells me to stay away so I don't influence my daughter farther down the road of sin. It's a slippery slope – it starts with drinking beer in public parks and leads to drinking wine on golf courses. What could be worse than golf course wine on a developing mind?

Forget it. I was done.

I saw my life story as it laid out in front of me, page after black and white page. I'd made a big mistake. I didn't blame anyone, but I'd made a mistake. I'd missed the life I was supposed to lead. I'd had a good life. I'd had a *great* life. I had a house, a job, a wife, a child. I had roots. But there was something missing – none of it felt like I'd earned it. It felt like it could all be whipped away whenever the Great Accountant in the sky realized there'd been a mistake in the ledger, and I'd never deserved anything this good.

Willie Brown was wrong all those years ago. Staying with Laura when she got pregnant wasn't my destiny. It wasn't me. Whoever the hell that was.

Up ahead, the tracks came to some kind of secondary highway. I looked back where I'd come from, and I couldn't see the lights of the city – not even as an orange glow underlighting the snow clouds. If I was this far out of town, I must have walked for a couple hours while mentally whining about how lucky I'd been to be blessed with a family. I let out a sharp blast of air through my nose. Fine. No more feeling sorry for myself. So what that I hadn't felt connected to anything – or anyone – I said I loved? What was I going to *do* about it? I wasn't going to be a divorce statistic. Hop on the next Greyhound out of town? Tempting. Still no.

The wind lashed my bare hands, and I stuck them into my pockets. I felt something small and hard and I pulled it out.

It looked like a chicken bone. But thicker – the thickness of a pork rib, but no longer than half my thumb. Honestly, if I had to guess, I'd say it was a finger bone. A human finger bone. I turned it around in my hands. It was heavier than it looked, and it was inscribed with chicken scratch markings. I assumed it was something from whatever tribe Willie Brown came from, but it almost looked Norse – like runes. What was I meant to do with it, again? Bury it at the crossroads, and I'll find what I'm looking for? Was that what he said?

Around me, the lines of my vision changed. Everything looked slightly off, as if the angles of perspective no longer lined up. One track never met up with the other in the distance. The snow felt hot on my cheek.

The same feeling I had talking to Willie Brown came back – that yearning for something better and mystical and perfect and unexplained. It's not like I believed this bone, buried at the crossroads, could change the way my life story turned out, but I was junkie-hooked on the perfect, mystical tingle in the back of my neck. I wanted to forget the fights with Laura, to forget Mak running off and forget teenagers overdosing and all of it. I wanted to just believe in weird old Willie Brown who showed up in my times of crisis. I wanted to believe in his little magic bone that would show me whatever it was I was looking for.

Do tracks and highway count as crossroads?

I dug a small hole with my toe through the gravel and into the cold dirt of the tracks, knelt down, dropped the bone into the hole and covered it with gravel. The wind picked up, and hit me with a sudden burst of cool ecstasy that started at my kidneys and radiated to my now numb fingers and toes, electrifying my nerve endings and steeling my skin against the cold and the wind.

That's when I saw him.

3. UP JUMPED THE DEVIL

"My man, my man, my *man*," the long-fingered man said when I'd finished my story. He walked toward me and twirled the toothpick in his teeth. "What a terrible night! I mean – that phone call. You've had *such* a rough go of it. How *did* you ever *survive*?"

"Fuck off," I coughed.

He looked to the darkened sky. "I knew I would be seeing you around these parts sometime soon. All y'all come to me eventually. Y'all want something for nothing. Let me guess – midlife crisis? Just turned forty? Woman troubles? Money troubles? I've seen it all, I've seen it all. Let old Papa Scratch help."

I gazed into the darkness and watched unfelt snow fall. I'd buried Willie Brown's bone. Now I wanted to play along and see where this went.

"Papa Scratch? What, like Old Nick? Like Satan?" I tried to sound matter of fact. Is there etiquette when asking if someone who appears before you was actually the devil or not?

He bowed low and gracefully, taking his hat off and swooping it in front of himself in a sweeping arc. "In the flesh, my man. In the flesh. And one of my favorite fleshes, to boot. You like?" He rubbed his hands along the length of his body, threw one hand on a hip, the other behind his head and puckered his lips.

I sputtered a not quite suppressed laugh.

"So, what – you've given up the spade-tipped tail and the Van Dyke and all that? To be honest, what you have going on now seems a little off brand."

Papa Scratch chuckled. "Hey, man, like anything in life, it's about making an impression. Goat horns and facial hair played well in the Middle Ages, but this is what puts the fear of God into them now." He gestured at his suit, his skin, at his long-knuckled fingers. I had to admit it was scarier than a guy in a devil costume.

I raised an eyebrow and pulled at my beard. "So – let me get this straight. I've summoned you at the crossroads to make some kind of deal? Is that about the long and short of it? This'll make a great story. I can really make Laura laugh with this one." If I were still talking to her. I missed making her laugh. "Seriously? The devil?"

"Ooh, we don't like it when outsiders use the D-word. That's our word. It's quite racist, really, but I'll let it slide with you. See – I like you, Wood."

Fine. He definitely knew my name. Didn't mean he was the devil himself.

"But just call me Papa Scratch. We're all friends here. And, yeah, you pretty much nailed it. I'm here to make all your wishes come true. I'm like your own personal little genie in a bottle." He waved one hand of those long crab leg fingers in front of his face in an old-fashioned stage magician gesture, waggled his eyes and flashed his grin.

I was skeptical.

"I'm skeptical," I said. I was trying, throughout this odd conversation, to keep the tingly, connected-with-the-universe feeling and the spiritual oddness of Willie Brown alive. I wanted to believe that I'd left the suburbs and walked into some kind of old blues song. I wanted to.

I didn't.

In fact, I'd taken too much on faith tonight. Hell, I'd taken too much on faith my entire life.

"Prove it." I was standing straight by now with my hands on my hips.

Papa Scratch took the toothpick out of his teeth and began passing it between finger and long finger. He was grinning broadly now. "Aw man, I don't play that way. I don't try out – I'm *varsity*. Like the man said, you either got faith, or you got unbelief. There ain't no neutral ground. You want to make a deal with me, let's make a deal. You want to walk the other way and go back to what's at home? Well I sho' nuff ain't gonna stop you."

No. Why was I even entertaining this idea? Something I could only describe as transcendent shriveled back into the hard little raisin turd it had been before I'd met Willie Brown. I felt more like myself.

I started walking away, listening as the flat crunch of gravel became only a sound now and not a symbol of where I was going like it had been just a few minutes ago.

The tinny tones of my phone in my pocket broke the sepia-tinged timelessness that had settled on the crossroads since Papa Scratch showed up in his old antique clothes with his old antique mustache. I didn't want to answer it. I knew who it was.

I answered it.

"Wood? Where are you? I thought you'd be home by now. Are you not going to help me deal with Makayla?"

"Look, Laura," I whispered, trying not to let this nut job who thought he was the devil hear something as mundane as a once-again-repeated argument with my wife. "You said you didn't want me around. I thought you were following the dictates of the Great Lemur in the sky, or whatever. I thought that's why you didn't even tell me Mak was back. I thought –"

"And *I* thought we were in this together. We used to be. Now I'm left to do all the heavy lifting." I heard a long, slowly exhaled sigh on the other end of the line. "You're not the man I married."

Those six words – an expression of the quotidian yet constant forces of spouse needling spouse – awakened an old, red primordial rage.

I didn't shout. I barely spoke above a whisper. "No. I'm not. I'm not the man you married. I'm the man you made me into." Without thinking or aiming or even wanting to, I threw my phone into the low brambles on the edge of the train tracks. It landed with a simultaneous thud and crack.

I was done.

I walked away from Papa Scratch back the way I came. Down a path I didn't want to walk anymore. I turned slowly. What could it hurt? What if he could show me what my life would've been? Didn't I owe it to my twenty-five-year-old self to find out? I wanted to play along and see where this went.

I crunched over the gravel back to the crossroads and stared into Papa Scratch's yellow eyes. "Okay," I said, still hoarse with emotion. "Let's make a deal."

Papa Scratch downright *twinkled* and waggled his willow fingers in delight. "Excellent, excellent. That's what I like to hear. So, tell me – what are you looking for? What strikes your fancy on this fine evening, my man? Is it fame? Riches beyond the dreams of avarice? Or just as much easy pussy as you can shake a phallic symbol at? I've got it all, I've got it all. And at the best prices you'll find this side of Babylon. So tell me, Woody, my man – what floats your boat?" His tongue popped out of his mouth and darted back and forth sideways across his lips. His toothpick fell to the ground.

I shoved my hands into my puffer jacket and felt acutely aware I was making a deal with the devil, and I wasn't even in my best pyjamas. I wanted to go home. Well, not really. I wanted to go to some safe place – the kind of place most people mean when they say *home*.

Papa Scratch pulled a long face and knitted his crab leg fingers under his chin. "Woody, Woody, Woody – you give up way too easily, my man. You can do better than that. C'mon – show me you got a little lead in your pencil. Tell me what you want. No need to be shy. I'm like a nurse – I heard it all." He smiled and steepled his fingers over his nose. "I just want you to be *happy*. That's my only little wish."

I thought about it. What *did* I want? What did I want bad enough to sell my soul to the devil? Those were the stakes, weren't they? My eternal soul? I wasn't sure what it was worth, but I'd be damned if I wasn't going to get a good price. So, what *did* I want?

I cocked an eyebrow.

I wanted to know. That's it.

I wanted to know what I would have been like if I had stood up and determined the course of my own life and not stuck with Laura when she got pregnant. I wanted to know who I could have been if I got to *choose* who I could have been. That was worth the price of my tarnished, dog eared soul, wasn't it? That's what I wanted.

"I want to know."

Papa Scratch looked at me expectantly, his mouth hanging open and his eyebrows high on his head. The words hung in the air, and his expectant face melted into confusion. "Know? You want to know something? What? Circumference of the earth? Airspeed of an unladen European swallow? The hidden secret to make any woman incredibly horny? I can let you know a lot of things."

"I want to know who I should've been. I just want to know what life would've been like if I hadn't listened to my Jiminy-Cricket conscience and done the noble thing."

Papa Scratch tilted his head back and laughed a low, throaty laugh. "I see, man. I see. You're looking for a simple life story alteration. Little snip here, little patch there. Presto! New life story. That's easy enough. It really is the most common thing y'all ask for, you know. More even than fame, power, the love of women. People just want to undo some decision they made, to tweak their life story, to correct those few degrees off that's now become a vast chasm." He waved his fingers in the air in the hackneyed magician's gesture again. "Yeah, I can do that."

I took a sharp breath in through my nose. "And what do I need to give you? My eternal soul or something?"

Papa Scratch walked around me like he was eyeing a cut of beef. He brushed his long fingers against my beard. In his eyes I could see the expertise of years appraising my worth. I watched him shift his weight almost imperceptibly from foot to foot. I couldn't tell what foot he landed on.

"Meh," he said, waving a hand at me. "I changed my mind. No deal."

My head snapped back. "No deal? What, my soul isn't sexy enough for you?"

Papa Scratch chuckled low. "Well man, I wouldn't have put it that way, but, yeah. Not *sexy* enough. You're a little too whitebread for me to do anything with." With his tongue, he flicked out another toothpick from what must have been the back of his throat and chewed it. "Well? Dismissed, soldier. I ain't got no more use for you."

I should've walked away. I was free and clear of this nutjob. This would have made a great story to tell Laura. But a little tickle at the back of my brain shouted *jump*.

"I need to know," I whispered.

He spat out his new toothpick. "Get outta here, man."

"Please," I said with a catch in my voice. "I need to know what would have happened if didn't give up painting."

He whipped out another toothpick from nowhere with his tongue, and his eyes lit up. "You an artist, Woody, my man?" His grin returned. "Well now, that *changes* things. See, I got a soft spot for artists." His yellow eyes shot up to the twilightening sky. "Okay, I like you. I'd just like to see you happy." He crossed his arms and something in his face darkened, causing his trim mustache to droop. "But it's non-returnable – you dig? Once you know, there ain't no way you get to un-know. But you wouldn't want that anyway, would you, Woody, my man?"

"No, no. I guess not. But I just want to see – to know. I don't actually want anything to change."

"Sure, sure" he smiled. "Just to know, Woody, my man."

I was trying to be careful with my words. If he honestly was the devil, any poor choice of phrasing would probably undo me. "Just to see what it would've been like if I didn't stay with Laura when I was twenty-five. I want to feel what it used to be like – I want to see if I could have kept that feeling alive." Was I starting to believe this little guy could do any of this?

"Sure, my man. Whatever you want."

"And nothing happens to Laura and Mak, okay?"

"Ha. Yep, everyone asks for that." He twirled his toothpick with his tongue.

"So … what do I have to do?" I felt the words catch in my throat and became suddenly aware of a waver in my knees.

Papa Scratch slit his yellow eyes and smiled wider. "Nothing, my man. Just come a little closer." He beckoned with one of his spidery fingers.

I was trying hard to believe in this. I knew all this couldn't *actually* be true, but I *needed* it to be true.

I stepped forward.

Papa Scratch reached out a long finger, touched me once between the eyes, and I flinched, then once on each of my shoulders. When he was done, he clicked his teeth together, stepped back and just stood there.

"That's it?" I asked.

"That's it. What – you were expecting more brimstone, maybe? A choir of angels to sing about your damnation? Nah, that doesn't happen. Not anymore. Do you know how expensive choirs of angels are these days?"

I expected more. I expected to feel like I'd made a mistake, or to be suddenly filled with some kind of open-heart-chakra warmth that would spread across my entire body and change my life. But I'd felt more while buying an extra pack of gum at the gas station to make the minimum for a credit card purchase.

"So ... how does it work?" I raised an eyebrow. "How will I find out if it worked? When will I know what I asked to know?"

"Heck, you're impatient. Offer a man what he's been waiting for all his life, and he won't wait a second more."

I didn't feel any different. I didn't know anything more than I did a few seconds ago. Crap. I guess he was just a nutjob, after all. I wanted something within me to change. I wanted to feel different. I wanted to feel *young*.

"So," Papa Scratch continued, distracted from an intense concentration. "I want you to just remember. Remember as hard as you can. Remember your life backwards, from this moment to the exact moment you made the decision that you now want to ball up and chuck away. Just walk through your memories as if they were paintings in a gallery. Can you see your way to doing that, my man?"

I found I couldn't do anything *but* remember, my memories came back in such vivid detail. I remembered tonight, the police coming to the door. Constable Santiago and her partner, Officer Scratch, in his old-fashioned suit. I remembered a conference I'd gone to a couple years back and sitting in the bar with the woman in a white dress and a red sweater. I *really* shouldn't buy her a drink. I bought her a drink, and Papa Scratch looked on from across the room and gave me the thumbs up. I remembered sitting with Makayla in my arms on the first morning of her life as Laura slept, and Papa Scratch and I watched the sun come up for the first time in Mak's life. I remembered standing at the front of the church on my wedding day and tripping over my vows, watching Laura smile at me in white lace and red flowers – she insisted on a red bouquet, the *feng shui* of it against her dress was too good for her to resist – and I watched Father Scratch's trim moustache under his broad, flat nose move and contort as he said the words that married us. And I wondered why he was wearing his hat at all, let alone on that jaunty angle, inside the church. I remembered standing naked in front of a blank canvas the morning after Laura told me she was pregnant. I'd known then that I'd give up painting, that I'd become *responsible*, but I wanted a swansong. I wanted one last work that would sum up who I'd made myself into over the years – Wood Sweeney, artist. I owed that to my unborn child. I owed that to myself. I wasn't able to even start.

And, strangely, there was someone else in the room. Why would I have been painting naked if there was someone else in the room? He stepped forward from the shadows, twirling a toothpick in his teeth, grinning broadly and pressing his long fingers together.

"You dig me, man?" Papa Scratch said, somehow simultaneously at the crossroads and in every one of my memories. "You feel me?"

"Something's happening," I said, and as I said it, I remembered saying the same thing naked in my studio, at the wedding altar, in the hospital, in the hotel bar and standing in my pyjamas outside my own house.

"I don't understand," I said, and it echoed through my memories. "This isn't what I asked for."

"Well, sure it is, boss," I remembered Papa Scratch saying as I stood with him in the cold in front of my house earlier that night. "A simple life story alteration," he said behind my shoulder as I talked to the woman in the white dress and the red sweater a few years ago. He grinned in the hospital room as Mak slept on my shoulder. He said, "Your story was sacrifice, man. You sacrificed yourself for your family. We're just having a lookee-loo at what it would've been like if you'd sacrificed yourself to yourself. If, instead of letting those ladies of your life feast on your psychic self, you used that energy and burned it into your art," he said as I stood naked in front of my last, still blank, canvas. I was slipping through memories fast now. "But first," said the Reverend Scratch on my wedding day as I gazed into

Laura's eyes. "We need to bundle up all the deadwood – all those useless memories that aren't going to do you any good once we're done our little snip-snip of your life story."

I was at the crossroads of highway and tracks. I was in the present. Maybe. I was on my knees with no idea how I got there. Papa Scratch towered above me and peered down with a glint in his darkened, yellow eyes.

"You know what? I really dig the fact that you're an artist, my man." There was only one voice now. "I got a thing for artists – any kind of artist. That's why I dress up in this one's flesh, to be honest." He stroked his cheek a few times with his knotted crab-leg fingers. "I'm going to sweeten your deal just a little bit more, Woody, my man. Yeah, man," he added, as if to someone else. "I like it, I like it. I just want you to be *happy*."

He clicked his teeth together three times again and clapped, wrapping long fingers around palms. Then he reached out and, magician-like, conjured something from behind my ear. But this was no coin. I saw its faint blue glow only for a second before he stuffed it into the pocket of his vest.

The points on my shoulders where he touched me started to burn, as if a smoldering cigarette were being crushed into each of them. But I didn't feel it for long. Soon the pain in my arms was drowned out by the pain in my psyche itself. I felt like I was falling – I flailed, and I think I smashed my hand against the cold steel of the train track. Memories were being torn from my head, and I could feel each one being ripped out, like slowly pulling off stale bandages. I could feel each point of contact between memory and mind snap and loosen.

It hurt.

I was left with gaping voids. I scanned my consciousness for the events of my life but found only emptiness and bleeding and pain.

And then something new entered.

In the holes of my life story, once filled with people I couldn't remember, I saw Papa Scratch dancing through the darkness, casting what looked like black sand from the pockets of his old suit. He was a devilish Johnny Appleseed re-sowing the desolate fields of my existence with people and places I'd never known. The falling feeling stopped, and I was left only with the intense vertigo of my life's needle skipping out of the groove and landing somewhere far away on another track.

I crumpled into everything that I'd been and done and collapsed at the crossroads of gravel highway and disused train line.

INTERLUDE

The man who walked, draped in fur, through this snowlashed mountain pass would eventually be known to the world as Ötzi when they found his preserved body. But that was many cycles away. Today, his people called him Weir Wihro. The wise man, the one who knows. They didn't know how he got so wise. They didn't ask. If they had, perhaps they'd understand why he had to leave the tribe. Perhaps they'd understand why he came up here to the mountains with only his furs and his copper axe. Perhaps they'd understand why he had to run away.

He didn't know how far he would need to go. Over the next range and into the next valley? Over all these mountains? It didn't matter. He would go. He had to. He would walk until the hide on his boots wore through, until the very skin of his feet wore through, to get away from the dark-skinned man of deals. To get away from the man he never should have talked to or bargained with. So Weir Wihro walked.

When Weir Wihro's seventh child was born – a girl – and died soon after of cold and hunger, he himself nearly died with her. He'd buried three of his children before, but something made this one different. He'd seen forty-three summers. He was an elder of the tribe. Why had he wept for the lost little girl? Why had his bones strained against the screams he kept inside himself, and why had he wailed and wept through the nights?

Like any father, he'd been worried about the future of his family, especially in this cruel winter, the coldest of the score he could remember. He'd gone to the shaman. He just wanted to see. He wanted to know what would become of him and his family in the future, down the dark unknown cycles of summers and winters.

But the shaman rejected him and told him it was not a man's privilege to lift the veil and look into the unfolding progression. That didn't make Weir Wihro happy. And because he was strong, and because he knew how to use an axe, Weir Wihro knew he could get the shaman to change his mind. The shaman was a weak little man, still beardless. And, as Weir Wihro expected, the new shaman cowered and broke at the sight of the axe and the thick arm that wielded it. He gave Weir Wihro a finger bone carved with strange lines and markings. The shaman said to take this bone to the place where the path of deer crosses the path of men and bury it. He would find what he was looking for.

Weir Wihro did as he was told. That's where he met the dark-skinned man of deals. That's where he was shown what waited for him, a horrific vision of death and eternal ice, of being trapped forever, unable to find his peace on the other side of the veil, unable to rest. And worse – his family, throughout the long cycles of summers and winters, would perish, would die and rot away from these mountains and from this world as completely and irreversibly as he would be forced to stay frozen within it.

No. It couldn't be true. He didn't want to know anymore. He wanted the vision gone. He'd wanted to return it to the dark-skinned man. He dug again into the cold ground, but he couldn't find the carved finger bone. He only saw the dark skinned man of deals. Weir Wihro demanded what he had before – he demanded his old life, free of the foreknowledge of his family's fall and of his own icy exile.

But the dark-skinned man just laughed. There was no way back.

And so Weir Wihro left behind his doomed family, left behind his tribe and walked into the mountains with only his furs, some berries, his fire pouch and his copper axe. The hounds were always close behind him. They wanted him. But he wasn't going to let them have him, or anyone in his family or tribe. And so he went to the mountains.

He heard the sound of cracking ice and looked around with reflexes well-tuned to the ways of these mountains. There was no sign of danger, and yet his heart pounded, threatening to shake apart the ice he stood on. Then he heard the long, sad howl from behind him – a sound that thrummed the bones of his back and seemed ready to tear open the veil between this world and the other side.

When Weir Wihro turned, the dark-skinned man was standing in front of him.

"Hey man," the dark-skinned man said as he brushed the falling snow from his odd clothes. "Ditching so soon? The party's just getting' started."

Weir Wihro didn't know what to do. The shaman – the old shaman, the one of the grey beard – had always warned the tribe about talking to the men from behind the veil, since they were possessed of great power. Weir Wihro didn't want to offend anyone possessed of great power. He gripped the yew handle of his copper axe tightly and cast his eyes to the ice beneath him.

"I thought we had a deal, my man. Why you running off? I don't think I like that. You've already seen the hounds, right? You feel me? You know what I'm saying, my boy?"

Weir Wihro squinted his eyes shut, but it didn't stop the visions of the hounds. He saw again the short black hair, the horse feet and the dead, bulging eyes. He heard the rattle of death again in the hound's throat.

"You are not going to like them one bit," the dark-skinned man continued. "Not one *bit*, my boy. They is going to rip you apart, still living, and carry you off to – what do you people call it? Beyond the veil."

Weir Wihro could smell urine, and he hoped he hadn't pissed himself in fear of the hounds. If he did, it would soon freeze and rob his body of the warmth he needed for his escape. But there was another smell mixed with it, a sharp smell that burned in his nose like the first sputterings of smoke on dry grass. He knew it was time. These were the smells of the hounds – the smoke, the sharp rot and the piss. The hounds were here.

Weir Wihro focused his fear into an evil eye of hatred and glared at the dark-skinned man. He felt a tear sting his cheek.

"Look, pal," the dark-skinned man grinned. "Don't put this on me. I gave you what you asked for. If you don't want it anymore, well, it's not like you can just give it back. There are rules about this kind of thing. You've seen too much, and because you even *tried* to unsee it … well, there are consequences." He looked to the frozen ground, strangely solemn. "There's nothing I can do for you now, man. You tried to undo our little deal. Now the hounds get to claim you. They get to make you one of them."

Weir Wihro heard the rattling breath of the hound behind him and felt his own urine wet his leg. He thought of his tribe and his family. He thought of his wife. And he thought of his little lost daughter, his Egda. He wept and turned to the hound, staring into its dead animal eyes.

It didn't hurt. At least not as much as he thought it was going to. The sooted needles the shaman had pierced him with to relieve the aches he had in his bones when the cold came hurt more. Death, he found, felt more like an unpleasant nothingness, a thorn in the bed that was bad enough to be felt in dreams, but not bad enough to wake.

Even when the hound, its hooves now elongated into sharp, skeletal fingers, wrenched out Weir Wihro's teeth, he only barely winced. When the fingers pierced his eyes and drained Weir Wihro's blood through the holes, he only shifted uncomfortably.

But when the hound swallowed Weir Wihro's soul – all the things of his life that made him the man he was – he howled. He howled the hollow howl, not of anguish – too late for that – but of desolation at his now endless existence.

They heard Weir Wihro's howl in the village, and they were afraid.

In the centuries that followed, Weir Wihro forgot his old body. He forgot his village, his lost little girl, and he forgot his name. The other hounds and the dark-skinned man called him only Pale, for his skin looked to be made of ice and snow and cold. His beard was gone now, and he'd cut off his hair. He liked it. He could see himself reflected in the terrified eyes of his victims, and he knew that he was Pale, the Soul Swallower.

4. I BELIEVE I'LL DUST MY BROOM

I felt something cold on my cheek, and I thought I was upside down. As I opened my eyes, I found that I *was* in fact upside down – face down on the hard, rusted steel of the track, my knees underneath me and my ass pointing awkwardly heavenward. Hm. Tequila.

"You done, my man?" Papa Scratch called to me from what sounded like miles away. And underwater. "Think we can get going soon? There's a scene I said I'd crash. And you need to be there."

I pushed myself up to kneeling and felt a whole lot worse for doing so. As I rubbed my cold-chapped cheeks with colder hands, I thought I might be forgetting something big. It was like the feeling of being unable to get at any details of a dream that was so life-changing in the minutes after waking. I shook my head slowly. But, like those dreams, whatever I was forgetting must've only *seemed* important by some trick of the mind or some obscure, mystical symbolism. I let it go. It wasn't like I could focus on anything right now, anyway. What did Papa Scratch say? Crashing another scene? Wasn't it time to call it a night?

"Another scene? I can't even remember the last one. Besides I should be getting home to ..."

"To what, man?"

"To ... to ... what's her name? And ... the other one."
Wow. I must've had more tequila than I thought. Did I make
a date for tonight? I felt like I was missing a sensation of
warmth and of unwanted belonging. Was I forgetting
something? *No*, a voice in the back of my brain shouted.

"Isn't it nearly dawn?"

"Dawn?" Papa Scratch grinned a broad grin, biting down
on his toothpick and making it point in a complementary
angle to his hat. "The sun's only just set, man. Now you
can't be telling me you're *that* far gone."

"No," I said. No, of course not. Just give me a minute."
I found the strength to stand up and dust off my pyjamas,
but found I was wearing a leather jacket and jeans. Just like
I always wore out. My trusty jacket. Pyjamas? What an odd
thought. I tugged on my beard.

"All right. I'm good. Where we going?"

"Oh, Woody, my man. You'll love it. It's just your cup
of poison." He spat his toothpick on the ground and tongued
a new one from god-knows-where. "C'mon. Get in the car."

I stood up and the gravel hurt my feet. No, it was the
boots that hurt. Their tight, black leather bit into my pinky
toes like a demon lapdog every time I even thought about
taking a step. Still, fashion above comfort, I guess. Pulling
my scarf tightly around my neck, I hobbled on bitten toes to
where Papa Scratch was half leaning on his bright, happy-
face-yellow Kia Rondo.

"Now, now, now Woody, my man." He wagged a crab
leg finger at me. "Get in – it's been decades since I had a
drinking buddy, and I know a place where there's a big
shindig going on. Do people say *shindig*?"

I was about to protest, thinking again that I needed to get
home. That someone was waiting for me. But I pictured my
empty apartment strewn with unfinished canvases and
finished bottles. There was nothing pulling me there.

"Fine. If you're buying," I said and pulled my woolen
flat cap down to my aching eyes.

Papa Scratch laughed his throaty laugh and started the car silently. I was starting to feel more like myself. I've got to remember to stay away from tequila.

We sat in silence for a long while. My thoughts were at odd angles with one another and needed a little time to settle, as if someone had shaken up a snow globe inside my head, and I couldn't see whatever chintzy Christmas scene was behind all the glitter.

"So ... you're the devil, right?" I said when I eventually said something.

Papa Scratch bounced his toothpick on his teeth. "Woody, my man, the D-word is racist these days. That's *my* word. But, yeah, man. That's who I am."

"Okay. So why do you drive a lemon-yellow Kia?" I thought it was a fair question. I would've pictured a black, seventies Cadillac with a flaming skull or something as a hood ornament.

"Woody, Woody, Woody," he chuckled. "Like I told you when we met – it's all about *impressions*. Nothing's ever about the truth, only about perceptions, deceptions and impressions. You know what would happen if I drove around in a big, black Cadillac with a flaming skull ornament? I'd have every two-bit, desert-living, mama's-basement, conspiracy-theory whackjob with a 3G connection out there telling the world they'd seen Satan himself. You think I want those kinds of people as my tribe?"

"Any publicity is good publicity." Whatever the right thing to say in this situation was, that wasn't it.

"Pub-*li*-city?!" Papa Scratch spat out his toothpick on the second syllable. "What do I want with *publicity*? None of us like publicity. Not me, not Thor, not Sasquatch. Certainly not the White Rabbit." He looked to the faded upholstery of the car roof. "Y'know, I really need to get those cats together for tapas again soon."

"You eat tapas with other demigods?"

"Well, what we eat depends on Sasquatch. He's the amateur chef. But more to the point, what would I want with publicity? I just want to be left in peace to do my good, honest work."

"Your work."

"Yeah, man. That's right. My *work*."

"And what's your work?"

He chuckled deep, blue and long, tossing his head back in a way I've only ever seen in the movies. "Just to make decent, ordinary folks happy. That's all I want out of life."

"And what have you ever done to make me happy? I'm usually the one buying the drinks."

Papa Scratch swerved the wheel to the right, narrowly missing an oversized SUV that would've made short work of his glorified golf cart. He stopped on the shoulder and glared at me, his yellow eyes wild.

"Do you even remember what you were like when I first met you? What was that – fifteen years ago? You were on the verge of making the worst mistake of your life. How do you think you would've turned out if you'd married that chick you knocked up? I'll tell you what it would've been like, man. It would've been a slow crucifixion. You'd have been nailed up and exposed to the winds of domesticity until you just shriveled up and crumbled to the dust that powders every un-lived life." He paused, still staring at me. He grinned suddenly and produced a new toothpick from somewhere in his mouth. "That what you want?"

Jesus. Laura. I hadn't thought of her in years. And the baby. He – or she – would be what? Fifteen now? I wondered briefly if the kid ever asked about me.

A sudden, forceful blow to the back of my head from Papa Scratch nearly knocked the cap off my head and derailed that morose train of thought. And none too soon.

"It's no time to get maudlin, man! We got things to *see*, people to *do*." He parked, got out and looked around. "I think a little fresh air will do you good, my man."

It did. The bracing air helped me collect my thoughts. I was Wood Sweeney. I was a painter. Not a terribly good one, but good enough to get by. I lived alone, but I was rarely without company. For whatever reason, women of a certain type were always exceptionally grateful I'd come into their lives. And it was downright impolite to argue with that gratitude.

The lobby of the hotel we walked into was large, marble and the kind of place I didn't think I could even afford to look at, let alone stay in. But Papa Scratch looked like he knew where he was going. He led us through a leather upholstered door and into a dim room, all fireplace, old oak and red Naugahyde. A jazz trio was playing a slow and mournful old blues. Papa Scratch put a drink in my hand. It was strong and sweet and licorice-y. I loved it. I loved life.

Illuminated on the white stucco walls of the bar were paintings – turbulent, hard-grabbing canvasses in shades of blue and black, with flashes of red and the whites of teeth and eyes. They were pieces full of human suffering – of wailing, of weeping, of the winnowing of a soul down to its barest. There were images of train tracks and of hounds and of old, dead trees, twisted in silhouette, the lynching noose never painted but always implied.

But there was a transcendence. There was a sense that the suffering *meant* something, that human beings, in the depths of their sorrow and their gnashing of teeth, could take hope that it was all for some sublime, perfect and knowable higher purpose. The canvasses felt like salvation. They felt like the blues the band was playing. I found they expressed with elegance something I'd always struggled with but had never been able to put onto canvas.

The band started a new tune. They'd added a sultry singer – a caramel-skinned, bleached blonde in a night-blue dress, her hair braided and twisted into tendrils that piled on top of her head and cascaded down in flirting carelessness. Her face and the illuminated canvasses were the only spots of light in the room. *The wind is hummin' through the churchbells, and the sky is turnin' pale* she purred as the bassline caressed the curves of her voice, and the piano vamped in chilled tones.

I caught myself staring at her, lost in the blue womanspeak of her voice. *Seem like every time I turn to go, there a hellhound on my trail.*

Papa Scratch put his hand on my shoulder and whipped out a toothpick from somewhere in his mouth. "I think she's got a thing for you, my man."

"What?" I felt myself blush a little. "No. She's just a good performer."

He chuckled low. "I bet she is. I *bet* she is." He drummed his spider fingers on his glass. "Good performer. Yeah. So how does it feel seeing your work on the walls?"

My work? I looked around at the canvasses, their blacks and blues of human suffering, and the transcendence that flowed from them. Of course. Of course it was my work. That tequila must've gotten to me if I was starting to forget my own canvasses. I'd gone to parts of myself I didn't know existed to paint this series. *Works in the Key of Blue*, I called them. I was glad I remembered that.

"I hear they've already sold five of the series." He downed his drink. "Come on, there's someone I want you to meet." He leered at me, his eyebrows rising and lowering several times in quick succession. "He's at the bar. I need a refill anyway."

The band started into a long series of deep blue, syncopated solos as we walked over.

I don't know what I was expecting, but I was not expecting this guy. Papa Scratch's leering had put an image firmly in my mind of someone with aviators, a spread collar and a medallion resting in his chest hair. What I saw instead was a young guy – twenty-five? thirty at the outside – clean-shaven with a short haircut carefully parted at the side, a pastel turquoise polo shirt and pleated khakis.

He bolted up from his stool when he saw me coming and held out his hand a good minute before I was close enough to shake it.

"Mr. Sweeney," he said, and I think his voice might've cracked. Or maybe I just imagined that because it went with the whole squeaky-clean package. "It's – it's so nice to meet you. I am a really big fan. Honest. Big fan." He'd been pumping my hand for the better part of a minute by the time he saw the look on my face and let go.

"Well, I'll let you two to your how-deedoos," Papa Scratch said. The leer he'd given me before had found its way into his voice.

I sat down at the bar beside – what was this guy's name? "Sorry – what was your name?"

"Me? Oh, right. I'm Braden. Braden Prendergast. Big fan."

I cocked an eyebrow. That was a good start. I was willing to play along and see where this went. I mean, if the guy's a fan, I guess I must owe him at least the time it took to down a drink.

I scrubbed the skeptical look off my face with a smile. "So, what can I do for you Mr. Braden Prendergast?"

He blushed deeper than the red Naugahyde of our barstools and took a long sip of whatever tangerine-colored concoction filled his cocktail glass. I drank in another look of the singer as he collected himself. *Leaves're fallin' like scattered ashes, and the bite is in the air.*

I caught a glimpse of Papa Scratch in the back corner, talking to two or three people. Normally, I wouldn't have given it a second thought, but there was something about the way he was holding himself. He seemed agitated, and his hat was pushed back on his head. He held his hands in front of his chest, palms out, stretching out his long fingers trying to subdue some kind of anger in the trio of people around him.

He was talking to a large black man, with a hat as old-fashioned as his own, and a pale white man, with short, pale blonde hair. A full-breasted, curvy-hipped woman with raven black hair looked on. The men looked angry. The large man in the hat kept pointing at something in my direction, then went back to stabbing his finger at Papa Scratch. The pale man licked his lips repeatedly, and I saw he had no teeth, only little grey slits where they once were. His eyes followed the big man's hands from where I was sitting and back to Papa Scratch. The black-haired woman, somewhere in her forties, had a kind of half smile – not a smirk or anything ironic – just a look that made it seem like she knew more than anyone else.

Papa Scratch had his hands up and was shaking his head *no*. The big man pointed again in my direction – was he pointing at me? Something about the body language of the whole scene suggested this was a quarrel that had been going on a long time. Everyone's gestures were angrily uncontrolled, yet they looked like they knew exactly how far they could go and went no further.

Anyway, none of my business. I looked to the blue-dressed singer again. *I need my man, my man, my man, to keep sweet company.*

When I looked back to Braden, his eyes were locked with mine.

"I feel that I may be honest with you as you are an artist." He had the steely resolve of somebody trying to conquer the knee-shaking, hand-sweating fears of social intercourse. "Yes, I feel that I may be honest with you. You see, it's my wife." His eyes fell to the bar. "I can't satisfy her."

I think my jaw might have dropped a little, and I cleared my throat into my glass as I sipped.

"It's fine," he continued. "I've come to terms with not being able to give her an orgasm. But, you see … I just think she *deserves* to be satisfied." He paused and looked away. "And I know that you can help me."

Could I? Was he talking about what I thought he was talking about? "I'm not sure what I can do," I said, still trying to lose the catch in my throat.

Turned out he was indeed talking about what I thought he was talking about.

"She has a thing for artists, you see. Artists are the only ones that ... that get her motor running. Is that the phrase? And I've tried. I've tried stretching canvas without a shirt on, smearing myself with gesso, even doing a Jackson Pollock-like painting on my, um ... privates. But nothing works. I just don't have any talent. And she needs the real thing." He leaned in and lowered his voice. "Will you do it for me?"

At that moment, he was half kid in candy store, half beaten-down dog waiting for the slipper to fall on his snout again. I had the feeling I wasn't the first artist he'd asked about this.

"Are you asking me to have sex with your wife?"

"Oh, no, no! I would never be so presumptuous." He stared at me without speaking as if I was supposed to chime in in response. I didn't. "But if you could give her an orgasm, I would really appreciate it," he added after a long pause.

Okay, now I was confused. I needed a bit of clarification about who'd being doing what to whose naughty bits. But I'd never learned the ins and outs of how to ask about that politely. "So – there wouldn't be anything in it for me?"

His eyes widened in freefall terror. "Oh! Of course, you *could* have sex with her. That would be great, too. But only if you wanted to." He cocked his head to the side as if just remembering part of his little sales pitch. "And don't worry – she's pretty. Here, I can show you a picture."

He fumbled in the back pocket of his khakis for an oversized wallet.

"Hold on, hold on. One thing at a time. Are you saying you would have no problem with me – someone you just met – making love to your wife? Have you thought this through? I mean you can't be more than what – twenty-five? You can't tell me you need to go to the nuclear option in your marriage already?"

Braden's voice lowered. Was he trying to sound older? "Mr. Sweeney, I truly appreciate your care and concern in this matter. I truly do. But I have talked this over with Melissa, and we are in agreement that a sexual liaison of some kind with a real artist – preferably yourself – would be extremely beneficial for our marriage."

Okay, how was I supposed to react to that? It's not like I *wanted* to cuckold the guy, but he was practically begging me to.

But, no. It was just too weird.

"Mr. Sweeney," he continued, slipping out of his grown-up voice. "You are of course our first choice. But, if you're hesitant, I have others I could talk to. I believe you know Colin Ackerman, the photographer?"

Fucker. He'd done his homework. He knew exactly how to push my buttons, bringing up that woman-beating weasel. Was I really going to do this? *Yes,* a voice in the back of my brain boomed.

"All right, fine," I chuckled, shaking my head a little.

"Yay! And don't you worry. She's only ever been with me. In a sexual way, I mean."

I took a long draught of my licorice-y drink and smiled into the glass. What the hell. I was willing to play along with it and see where it went.

"Oh, there's one more thing, Mr. Sweeney. Do you … do you think I could watch?" The words hung in the air for a moment. He must have seen in my reaction that I didn't quite take it as he meant it. He added quickly, "Not for any kind of kinky reason, of course. I just … I just, you know, I want to see how you do it. To see how an artist does it. So maybe I can learn to do it myself. To make logistics easier, I've already booked a room in the hotel upstairs. Just in case you said yes."

He scribbled a room number and a phone number on his napkin, and gave it to me.

Taking on his co-conspiratorial tone again, he leaned into me. "Maybe, if it works out, we can make this a regular thing? Give us thirty minutes to get everything in order. Then just knock on the door." He shook my hand again until the fading of my smile made him break away.

For some reason, I was actually starting to like the guy. Or at least respect him. I could get behind the fact that he was willing to do anything it took, no matter how unselfish, for his wife.

Or he just got off on watching.

I turned around on the stool and looked back to the singer. *If my baby refuse me, man, he ain't gonna put it right.* If I didn't know any better, I'd think she was giving me the eye. But I knew that with the spotlight on her, there was no way she could see me all the way over here. And yet there was something about her, a presence and intensity that made it sound like she was staring straight at me, singing right to me. *Take my HR handygun, tell him to say goodnight.*

Papa Scratch sat down beside me. "Bartender? How about a papa scratch for me and my friend?"

The shaven-headed waif behind the bar raised her eyebrows quizzically.

Papa Scratch rolled his eyes and pulled a toothpick out from somewhere in his mouth. "Spiced rum and anise liqueur. That's a papa scratch." He leaned toward me. "I'm trying to make it a thing. I think I'm getting close."

I sipped the papa scratch quickly. I had thirty minutes to kill, and a pretty stiff buzz to get on if I was going to be able to do what I'd just agreed to do. Or at least do it without a skeptical raised eyebrow the whole time.

Papa Scratch clicked his teeth together and smiled.

5. HONEYMOON BLUES

The fluorescent light in the elevator buzzed in harmony with the humming of the booze in my blood. Was I seriously going to make love to another man's wife just because he practically begged me to? *Yes*, the voice in the back of my brain said. I told myself I was just going to see how everything played out.

As I walked through the unforgiving light of the hall, I yanked my woolen cap down low, pulled my scarf tight around my neck and knocked on the Prendergasts' door more timidly than I meant to.

Braden Prendergast opened the door a crack and let me in. He was still wearing his turquoise polo shirt. And nothing else. His pale, hairless legs carried him over to a couch across the room where a small brunette in a silk robe sat on her heels.

Prendergast was right. The missus was pretty. But small. She had a China doll quality about her.

"Melissa, this is Mr. Sweeney. The *artist.*" Prendergast was pouring drinks from a stand at the far wall. "He's been kind enough to agree to help us out."

"I'm very glad to meet you, Mr. Sweeney," she said in what sounded like a fake husky voice. She smiled, stood up and blinked a couple times, maybe in an attempt to bat her eyelashes. "I just *love* your work." She cast her eyes down to her knees. "It makes me wet."

"Well, always happy to meet a fan," I deflected as she stood too close to me. "And please, call me Wood."

Her eyes shot back up on me again. "Wood," she purred. "Good. I need to make sure I scream the right name." As one hand pushed my cap to the back of my head, the fingers of her other hand ran up my arm to my neck and felt the weave of my scarf. With a snap, she pulled it off me and hung it on her own neck, bringing it to her nose and breathing deeply.

Prendergast put a glass of something brown in my hand, and I rattled the ice cubes in it. "Well, I will leave you two to get acquainted. I will be in the bathroom if you need anything." His eyes scanned the room. "Honey, have you seen my e-reader?"

"I think you already put it in the bathroom, sweetie." The coquettishness was gone, and she spoke to her husband exactly as anyone would about the mundane, day-to-day things that make up a life. "You wanted to get everything ready before Mr. Sweeney – before Wood got here."

"Oh, thanks, hon." He bent over and pecked her on the cheek, and his ass peeked out saucily from under his polo shirt.

I was left alone with Melissa. She eased back onto the couch and patted the cushion beside her for me to sit down. I did.

"So," she purred again in her practiced bedroom voice. "Tell me about what you like."

I took another sip of whatever I was drinking. There was a seductive acid bite that softened and smoothed the sting of the booze. "Right now, I really like this drink."

She giggled girlishly. "I taught Braden how to make them – I learned from a magazine. It's spiced rum and anise, then you put a little squeeze of lemon that you burn a bit with a lighter. It's nice, isn't it?" She took a sip of her own and cast her eyes down again. "Speaking of squeezing lemons …"

"Hm, I'll have to remember that. I think I like the way you younger generation take the time to do things the old-fashioned way."

"You may like a lot of things girls of my generation can do." She took a breath as if ready to say something, but I interrupted her.

"Well I certainly like the drinks."

She let the breath out slowly. I sat a lot more rigidly than I would've expected. I could feel the warmth from her body on my shoulder, but I didn't lean in. I sat with one hand on my knee and the other taking sips of my drink far more frequently than was natural.

"So," she exhaled. "Tell me about the creative process. Does the fit come on you slowly and softly, or does it burst out of you in wave after wave of sensual release?"

I'm not sure I'd ever thought about it in those terms. I didn't know what to say. "Um, I guess it depends on the painting and the idea that it comes from. Some of them come out pretty much fully formed, but some I need to tweak over the course of months. I'm afraid it's not all that exciting." I raised an eyebrow. Why was I trying to sabotage this? Was I seriously cock blocking myself right now?

She put her hand on my thigh and leaned in. "I find it exciting." She put her drink down beside her and her lips up to my ear. "My panties are soaked," I think she said, but all I heard was hot breath.

"Hm," I said and took another sip.

We sat in silence for what felt like about fifteen minutes, her eyes sizing me up and mine glancing awkwardly around the room and back to my drink, which was empty now. "You mind if I, uh, freshen this up?"

She closed her eyes, sighed, then looked at me and smiled. "Sure," she said. "But get Braden to do it. He'll do the thing with the lemon that you like." She turned and called out her husband's name exceptionally unerotically.

His head popped out of the bathroom. "Yes, my love?"

"Wood wants another drink. He likes the lemon."

"Yes sirree. Anything you need. Wood, why don't you come over here, and I'll show you how I make them?"

I sprang off the couch faster than I probably should have and regretted it. I didn't want to hurt anyone's feelings.

The essential absurdity of standing beside a man wearing only a polo shirt as his wife was trying to seduce me began to sink in. I was pretty sure I'd never truly understand Braden and Melissa's relationship, so I just held out my glass for the man to fill and felt conspicuously overdressed in my leather jacket and woolen cap.

Without looking at me, Braden spoke under his breath, as if he didn't want his wife to hear or even realize we were talking together. "Hey, Wood. I hate to be a bother, but do you think we could move this along a little bit? As long as you're comfortable with that. It's just that I have a client meeting in the morning."

Right. I wasn't used to having husbands tell me to hurry up and slip it to their wives. It was a lot of pressure.

"I know you're doing most of the ... heavy lifting in this situation," Braden continued in his whisper. "But, I think as ... supplier, I guess, I have a few rights in the transaction, as well. Seriously, would it be okay if you guys just started?"

The way he phrased it as a business deal either made me feel better about the whole situation or a hell of a lot worse. Not for the first time that night, I didn't know what to say.

"I guess," I said, feeling like a scolded adolescent. "Hey – are you sure you're okay with all of this?"

He turned to me stony faced and put the drink in my hand. "Yes," he said deadpan. "It was my idea, wasn't it? Now I'm going to go read my book for about five more minutes. After that I'll come out, and I'd really like to see ... well, you know."

Fine. This was just too weird to argue with. If I was going to do it, I was going to do it. I didn't want to keep second-guessing Prendergast's motives or feelings or whatever.

I heard the bathroom door close, and when I turned around, Melissa was standing behind me, naked save for my scarf around her neck. Her small, dark nipples were hard and pointed, and I saw gooseflesh on her thighs.

Without saying anything she walked toward me, got down on her knees and unbuckled my belt. She gazed into my eyes as she undid my jeans and pulled them down to my ankles. I stared into my drink and had another sip.

She knitted her eyebrows and pouted her lower lip. "Tell me what it's like when you paint," she said and took me into her mouth.

I wanted to oblige. I really did. It seemed only fair. It's just that when I painted, I just started off, then got into the zone or my mind went all Zen or something, and *there!* I had a painting. But since she was doing what she was doing with such enthusiasm, I figured it was only polite to say something. So I made it up.

"Well," I said gasping a little. "First, I pick up the brushes, and feel the stiffness of their bristles against my skin." Her muffled moan suggested that was the kind of thing she was looking for. "And then I – slowly – squeeze the paint onto my palate, staring into its color and breathing in its sharp, chemical scent. And then I, on the canvas, with my, I don't know."

She must've heard enough. Holding my gaze, she stood up, wiped her lips with the back of her hand and pushed me onto the bed. My leather jacket creaked and squeaked.

She tossed me a condom and I ripped it open, fumbling to find which side was up. She watched my bungling for a few seconds, took the thing from me and placed it gently in her mouth. The "O" of her lips made her look uncomfortably like a sex shop blow-up doll, but that image dissolved – everything in my head dissolved – as she slid the thing onto me slowly and smoothly with her mouth. Where do people learn how to do these things? Then, in a motion, her tiny frame straddled me, and she guided me inside of her. I closed my eyes and tried to enjoy the experience, tried to put aside the strange circumstances that brought it about. I was half successful. As long as I kept my eyes closed.

They say you can tell there's someone else in the room because of a subtle change in temperature caused by body heat. I don't know I would've been able to detect a subtle temperature change with the other sensations I was experiencing, but I knew someone else was in the room.

I opened my eyes. Braden Prendergast was poised awkwardly half bent over so he could kiss his wife. He'd lost the turquoise polo shirt and was now completely naked, his bulbous-headed erection pointing almost accusatorily at me.

"Hey Wood," he said as casually as if we'd met in the canned goods aisle of the supermarket or anywhere else where I didn't have his naked wife riding me. "Sorry, I hope you don't mind. I've been watching for a little while – and I very much appreciate you giving me this glimpse into your technique. I just thought I would join in for a little bit. We could work together. You wouldn't mind that, would you?" He didn't give me a chance to answer.

In a motion, he was on the bed, squatting behind his wife and entering her anus. I could feel him slide in.

"You like that," he croaked without a trace of his usual nervousness. I assumed he was talking to Melissa. He wasn't. "Yeah, you like that. You like feeling my cock rubbing against yours through my wife." I heard the tinny click of a camera phone. "This is going on our Instagram, for sure," he grunted.

Right. This had gone far enough. Maybe it had gone far enough quite a ways back, but watching his clean-cut head thrown back as he and I crossed swords deep in his wife's pelvic floor – that was the end of it. I was done. I tried to wriggle out from under the Prendergasts, but every move I made was met by the bucking of her hips and his gasps of pleasure. I realized suddenly that, in my forty years on this planet, I'd never had the need to escape from underneath a naked married couple, and I found I had no natural skill for it whatsoever.

How was I going to do this without being rude?

She reached out a hand and dug red-manicured nails into the flesh around my nipple. I saw my chance.

"Ow, ow, ow," I shouted, hoping it sounded real enough, and, with main force, rolled onto my side clutching my chest with my hands.

Mrs. Prendergast was forced to dismount by clumsily falling backward into her husband, which must have forced him into her at an awkward angle. She took a sharp breath of air through her teeth and probably clenched at the source of the pain, because Prendergast yelped like a ... well, like a man who just got his penis clamped down on in his diminutive wife's rectum.

When we all had our anatomies back to ourselves again, neither of the Prendergasts looked very happy.

"Look, I'm sorry," I said as I grabbed my pants and boots. "It's just that I have bad case of areolar dyspathy. Always have."

"What in God's green is *areolar dyspathy*?" Prendergast half-shouted.

Did that not sound medical enough? "It's an oversensitivity of the nipple. It actually affects about one in twenty people who –"

"I don't need to hear any excuses, mister," he snapped. "You, sir, are a famous artist and as such, you have a responsibility to your public. We have been nothing but courteous to you, and how do you repay us? You have left us both extremely aroused and without release. Is this how you treat all of your fans? Don't you walk away from me! Get back here and make my wife come!" He paused. "Don't you even want your scarf?"

I ducked out into the hall, pantsless, banking on the Prendergasts not following me out while still completely naked.

I took a moment to breathe once in the stairwell. I don't think they were following me. In fact, I think I might've heard Mrs. Prendergast's muffled ecstatic screams. Huh. She was certainly enjoying her husband a lot more than he said she did. Good for him.

I was happy it worked out for those two, but never got to bask in the sentiment. I became reddeningly aware of my current lack of pants. I fumbled to get them on as quickly as possible, falling into the concrete wall as I did. It was a bit of a delicate operation getting the zipper up – my mind, my conscience, even what was left of my dignity may have decided I was done with Mr. and Mrs. Prendergast, but, as usual, my cock had a completely different idea and still pointed determinedly in their direction.

I thought about going back to the party downstairs but decided against it. Being this horny in a room full of art groupies – at my own show – would probably lead me to some bad decisions. *More* bad decisions. I should set a limit of one bad decision per night.

When I got downstairs, I took in the marbled opulence of the lobby for a moment to try to keep the barking beast in my pants at bay. It didn't help. All I could see were the forms of breasts and hips, asses in tight-fitting dresses, legs carrying female forms high-heel clicking across the marble. I went to the washroom and turned on the cold tap, splashing a little on my face.

I looked at myself in the mirror, and eyes looked back at me that seemed to know so much more than I did. That had seen things I hadn't. That had lived a life I'd never lived. Or maybe that's what all eyes in mirrors looked like. Maybe that uncanny feeling of staring into an all-knowing soul was just a trick of the brain's facial recognition.

A voice in the back of my brain shouted *now*.

Not knowing what the probably-crazy, phantom voice wanted, I stepped out of the washroom.

Slinking through the plush-carpeted hotel hallway with an unlit cigarette in her painted lips was the brassy, macramé-haired, jazz band singer.

Now, the voice shouted again.

"No!" I hiss-whispered at the voice and regretted it when she turned to me, casting her eyes from side to side.

She took a step forward. "You're the artist," she said, and it sounded like singing. "The one who did all of those dark, sexy, glorious paintings out there, right?"

The water dripped off my face and onto my shirt. For a second I didn't know what she was talking about. I'd given up painting a decade and a half ago when … when. No, that was wrong.

"Yep, that's me," I said, and it sounded nothing at all like singing.

"I *love* your work." She closed her eyes and bent her knees slightly as she caressingly drew out the word *love*. The water dripped off my face. "Something about the thread of light, the lifeline of human dignity that you present through all of the blackness and the grey days of everyday existence. That's what I try to do in my own small way. In my music."

With liquid accuracy, she shifted around me into the washroom. She reached out, grabbed a paper towel and gently blotted my face. She smelled of early summer and evening and hopefulness.

"And you do," I said a little too loudly for how close she was to me. "I mean, the songs – and the way you sing them – very … thread of light." I tried to look away from the candy apple of her lips and the sweep of black at the corners of her dark eyes that elongated them to into an almost feline elegance. I tried to look away. I didn't.

"My heart's beating fast," she said, putting my hand on the soft skin of her chest. It was beating fast. "I think it's being this close to you," she breathed. "I looked at your work tonight, and I wanted to *be* you. I wanted to be inside of you. Or at least have you inside of me. Can I be completely honest with you?" She didn't pause for an answer. "Your work turns me on."

"Does it?" was all I could think to say, cocking an eyebrow. "I'm not sure I believe that."

She took a step back and folded accusatory arms in front of her.

"You don't believe me? You want proof?" Her tone had lost its smooth seductiveness, and there was a sharp, new edge to it.

"Fine," she sighed in mock resignation and turned around, walking to an empty stall with an exaggerated sway of her hips.

Hm. If it seems too good to be true, it probably is, right? But the sheer volume of adolescent fantasies that had been fulfilled tonight – selling my canvasses, the Prendergasts, this singer – kept me playing along to see where this went. I felt the elastic could snap at any minute and I'd be sent hurtling back to some kind of drab, oatmeal existence, but not yet. I pushed my cap to the back of my head.

"You want proof that your paintings turn me on? She shimmied the blue dress up her hips, put her foot on the lid of the toilet and pulled aside her shimmering black panties.

Well. *Something* excited the young lady, and who was I to say it wasn't my work? What was it with women and painters tonight? It seemed like I was finally getting the kind of perks my musician friends had always enjoyed. It almost seemed too good to be true.

But as my erection surged against my zipper rather uncomfortably, I thought of Braden and Melissa Prendergast.

"You don't have a husband watching us from somewhere, do you?"

"I don't have a husband at all," she said, and it still sounded like singing. But with a lot more blue notes.

This was a bad idea. I shoved my hands into the pockets of my leather, and one of them scraped against a condom. It made a noise that sounded like a voice in the back of my brain shouting *yes*.

Call me weak. Call me typical and predictable. Call me a beast. But those were *my* canvasses out there, my work, my effort. This was *my* show. I toiled to get here, and now it was my turn to reap the rewards. Basically, it was my party and I'd screw if I wanted to. At that moment, it was the best bad idea I ever had.

I unclenched a face I didn't know was clenched, and with that act, I slipped from my self-imposed ties of *should* and *shouldn't* into the ironclad, gravitational pull of the moment. Something old and tight, some forgotten tensed muscle somewhere down in the back end of my fundament slacked and released, sending me slipping toward the singer in the blue dress, slipping into her mouth, into her body, into her very story.

As I rode on the wave of my pent-up potency, I was Zeus, I was Odin. I was a god unto myself, giver of pleasure, and receiver of offerings. My whole body became pure thrust, and the singer I didn't know the name of became an extension of me, as I became an extension of her, and we moved together, each balanced on the thread of light that penetrated the grayness of our own lives, each part of the other, unified, holy, yet inescapably alone.

Then I had a vision of her parents, proud that their little girl was making a living doing something she loved as much as singing.

I thought of my abandoned son or daughter. Fifteen years old now.

I slowed down my pace. "Does your father know you do things like this?" I asked.

"Ex-fucking-cuse me?!" she snapped, pulling away from me and shoving me into the stall door. My cap fell off the back of my head and landed neatly in the toilet.

6. TRAVELING RIVERSIDE BLUES

She wrenched herself past me and put herself back together. "What the hell is wrong with you?!" she said with none of the musicality that danced through her voice just a few minutes before.

She stormed out of the stall, triggering the motion detector for the automatic flush. I stood alone as the empty toilet swirled and sucked with its industrial force, but it was no match for the wet wool of my formerly favorite cap. The water overfilled the bowl and pooled around my shoes. I figured I should pull up my pants. Was this honestly who I was at forty years old?

I went to the sink, washed my hands and splashed some more cold water on my face, this time careful to blot it off myself. I drank in my own reflection, saw the lines, saw the deep purple under my eyes, my raised eyebrow skeptical at even myself. Maybe it was time for a change.

Tomorrow.

I headed back to the bar to have another drink.

As I clacked through the grand marble of the lobby, something made me look over my shoulder. I didn't see anything out of the ordinary. I just saw the door ajar to the plain, staff-only hall that led to another door with a red exit sign burning above it. A voice in the back of my brain shouted *go*.

I figured I'd see where it went so walked through the little door and down the white tile hallway of the old hotel to the door with the exit sign.

I pushed it open and found Papa Scratch there. And he wasn't alone.

I took in the scene quickly and the hairs on the back of my neck stood up immediately. Scanning the alley, I saw Papa Scratch. His hat was lying on the dirty snow beside him. Directly in front of him – right up in his face – was a large, quarterback-looking guy with coiffed hair and a necklace made of little shells or coral or something that matched perfectly the pale orange of his polo shirt.

Behind Kenny the quarterback was a little waif of a blonde girl who didn't look a millisecond over fifteen. The plunging of her neckline gave her a dressing up in mommy's clothes look. Her lips were trembling in the harsh, white light of the service dock.

Kenny the quarterback was barking. "I said – What's. Your. Fucking. Problem?" He stabbed his finger into Papa Scratch's shoulder with every word. "You think a fucker like you gets to even go near a girl like that? Let alone have his hand in her goddamn pants?"

Papa Scratch was smiling and tossing the toothpick with his tongue from one side of his mouth to the other. "Hey, man – don't get all up in *my* face about it. Why not ask the young lady if she had any complaints? It looked to me like she was having a better time than she could with some white bread, corn fed, pigs in a blanket, milk boy like you. I got the *knack*, you see." Papa Scratch stuck his tongue out and flitted it under Kenny the quarterback's nose. His toothpick fell to the ground.

I didn't even see Kenny raise his fist and wind up. I just heard the hard, meat-slab sound of that fist connecting with Papa Scratch's jaw, and the scream from dressed-up-in-mommy's-clothes.

Papa Scratch staggered back, and Kenny covered the distance between them in a step. "Walk away, old man. You don't want to do this."

"Old?" Papa Scratch said, rubbing his jaw. "I look old to you? This skin was only thirty-six when I took it over. And I think I've kept it in perfect working order. At least your girlfriend said so."

Kenny gave Papa Scratch a two-handed shove. "Stay. The fuck. Away. From. Her."

Papa Scratch still grinned. "Aw. Now how am I supposed to do that? When she tastes so good just like a young girl should." He ran his fingers under his nose and licked them.

The quarterback's face up until now had been a fist-shaking, angry red. Now, the color drained out of him, and his shoulders dropped. His whole body slackened, shedding its coiled anger. He looked, I imagined, exactly what people look like right before they murder someone else in a crime of passion. I swallowed several times.

Should I help him? I mean, he was the devil – why had I never thought about how weird that was until tonight? – but Kenny the quarterback looked ready to kill. Too late.

Kenny swung, Papa Scratch bobbed, and it missed him. The first time. Regaining his balance and smirking, Papa Scratch had put too much effort into being cocky to notice that Kenny had another fist, this one on a collision course with Papa Scratch's nose.

It connected with a thick crack, and Papa Scratch went down hard, like a snipped-string puppet.

Kenny the quarterback looked like he was almost more surprised at felling his opponent than Papa Scratch was at being felled. His eyes had lost their murderous hardness and were now open wide in surprise, and he flailed his splayed hand in pain.

This was probably a good time for me to step in.

I inserted myself bodily between quarterback Kenny and the fallen Papa Scratch. The pounding of my heart in my throat scared away any moisture there, and no sound came out when I first tried to speak.

"Hey, hey. Come on. Please," was all I could manage to get out once I'd found my voice. "He didn't mean it, I'm sure. How about he just apologizes to you and your – girlfriend? sister? – and we'll call it a night? How would that be?"

"I don't know," Kenny sputtered. The momentum behind his attacks had spent itself, and I thought he'd be looking for a way out. I had no idea if Papa Scratch could be killed by the likes of this troglodyte, but from the looks of his crumpled body, he could certainly be hurt. And for some reason I felt like I owed him something, more than just the general human sense of not wanting to see an acquaintance beaten to a bloody pulp.

"Yeah, it'll be good," I went on. "He'll just apologize for whatever offense he's caused – and believe me I know what kind of offense he can cause – and we'll just all be on our way in whatever separate directions this night might take us. How does that sound?"

Kenny looked at the blonde, and she nodded. The color came back to his face. "All right," he said slowly. "But he better fucking *mean* it when he says sorry."

I gave the kid what I hoped looked like a knowing nod. "I'll make sure of it," I whispered.

Papa Scratch took my offered hand, and I pulled him up. His mouth and chin were bloodied, and his crisp, white shirt was stained with large splotches of red. His eyes had turned a deeper yellow.

"You're going to give the nice gentleman a proper apology now, aren't you?" I cocked my eyebrow and squeezed his arm.

Papa Scratch grinned. "Oh, yes massa," he said in a broad southern accent. "I's so very sorry, massa. I won't be lookin' at no white woman again, massa."

Kenny took a step forward, but I puffed up my chest just a little and held his gaze. He backed down. I gambled on him not wanting to kill a man with his bare hands tonight.

"Come on," he said to the blonde and grabbed her hard on the arm. I felt bad. I'd prefer Papa Scratch get the living shit kicked out of him than anything happen to that little girl. But I watched them walk away, and The acid rose in my gut.

Papa Scratch spat a mixture of spit and blood dramatically on the ground. I dropped his arm and smacked him on the back of the head. "What the hell do you think you're doing?"

As we walked back through the hotel's service entrance, Papa Scratch wiped his face and dabbed his lip with a rapidly reddening handkerchief. "I suppose you'll be looking for me to thank you or something. Is that right?"

Yeah, that was exactly what I wanted. Of course, I knew I wasn't going to get it from him. Papa Scratch had a lot of good qualities – not any that I could think of at the moment – but humility and gratitude weren't among them.

I just shrugged. "Can you even be hurt? I mean, how long have I known you? Fifteen years? How come I don't even know if you can be hurt?" I left out the bigger and perhaps more important question of why I was so accepting of the fact that I was friends with the devil himself. I'd taken everything at face value about Papa Scratch for this long, and tonight all the questions came up.

"Yeah, man. I can get hurt," he said spitting out some more blood and whipping out a new toothpick with his tongue. "Heck, I could even get killed." He took the handkerchief away from his face and stared at me with his yellowed eyes. "Shit, man. I could've gotten *killed*. I guess I owe you one there."

"Forget it. Just try to stay out of trouble, okay?"

"No, no, Woody, my man. You did me a real solid. I never carry a debt. Here." He fished into the side pockets of his old double-breasted suit and pulled out a large, silver coin. "This ain't nothing but a token, but it shows that I owe you one. To be repaid when and where you see fit. You saved my life – you get one unrefusable favor from me."

I chuckled a bit. I knew Papa Scratch – he wasn't about to do anything he didn't want to do, magical coin or no magical coin. But he was so damn earnest about the whole thing, so I held out my hand took and his coin. I looked it over quickly – it had a rough, low relief of some king I didn't recognize on one side, and a hastily carved goat on the other. I stuffed it in the pocket of my leather and went to look for some paper towels or something for the blood that wouldn't stop dripping from Papa Scratch's now slightly bent nose.

"One unrefusable favor. From me," he said again.

I was already far enough down the white tile hallway that I didn't feel the need to respond.

Once we got him cleaned up, Papa Scratch snapped quickly back to his old self. He started telling me, in lurid detail, what he had been planning to do to Kenny the quarterback's girlfriend. And it made me blush. Me, who just tonight had my cock up another man's wife while he watched, I flamed scarlet at the things that guy had in mind.

"Damn! I is hungry. You hungry? You wanna get a little something?" Papa Scratch looked at me and grinned too broadly. There was some kind of subtext behind all of this, but I had no idea what it was. So I played along with it to see where it went.

"I could eat," I shrugged. My head was cold.

Papa Scratch clapped and rubbed his hands together. "Alright, alright. I know just the place."

We walked a little along the River Landing. They'd done it up nicely here. In the last few years it had become no longer just a dumping ground for the drunks and the junkies. *Gentrified* was the word. I hadn't been down here much, but

I was happy they cleaned it up, especially since I had a fifteen-year-old daughter. What? No, no. *If* I had a fifteen-year-old daughter, I'd be happy they cleaned it up. What an odd thing to think.

We'd left downtown now and were starting to make our way through the winding streets of the vinyl-sided suburbs.

"You think anything's going to be open around here? Why don't we head back to town and get a hot dog or something?" I said.

"Hot dog!" Papa Scratch laughed, and the toothpick fell out of his mouth. "Hot dog – I love it, man. I love it."

We didn't turn around. He led me to the empty parking lot of a little strip mall, its storefronts black and its signs promising ice cream, eyewear and dry-cleaning barely visible in the midwinter blackness.

Papa Scratch walked up to one of the glass doors and knocked rhythmically, as if it were a secret code to get into a nineteen-twenties speakeasy. I looked at the sign – *Pounce 'n' Play Pet Store*. No. Come on. He wasn't going to –

Papa Scratch knocked again, and this time there was shuffling from the other side of the door. A bolt clicked heavily and the door opened a crack. I couldn't see who was on the other side.

They spoke in a language I didn't understand. Ukrainian maybe? It was a soft language, yet heavy and throaty. It sounded like the swish and splash of wet slush on the first warm day of spring. Papa Scratch seemed to be arguing with the woman on the other side of the door – at least it sounded like arguing, and at least it sounded like a woman. No, not *arguing*. Bargaining. Haggling. They both started to make sounds of agreement, and Papa Scratch smiled.

Then I heard the yelp.

Passed through the open door and into Papa Scratch's long, bony fingers was the little tan furball of what I guessed was a golden retriever pup. The rest happened so quickly that I could only think of one word.

No.

The dog barely made a sound as Papa Scratch bit into it. I wish I could've said the same for him, and though it happened too fast for me to think about turning away, it wouldn't have made a difference with all the slurping and sucking.

In a few seconds it was over, and Papa Scratch was licking his long fingers. He walked over to the trashcan, wiped his mouth with the blood-sodden hide and carefully tossed it out.

"What?" he smiled at me. "You didn't want some, did you pal o' mine?"

I walked home after Papa Scratch ditched me for the next ya-gotta-be-here party, and I tried to make sense of the night. But nothing added up. I had a double handful of puzzle pieces scattered around the table of the last twelve hours, but I didn't think they were from the same puzzle. Was this who I was? Every time that question came up in my mind, the voice at the back of my brain shouted *yes*, but it shouted so forcefully that I was having trouble believing it. I wondered about people who had been hypnotized to cluck like a chicken at the snap of someone's fingers. I wondered how it worked. Did they, when they heard that hypnotist's snap, have a voice in the back of their brains that shouted *okay, now cluck like a chicken*? Was this the same kind of thing? Had I been hypnotized into thinking that I was the kind of man who'd agree to satisfy another man's wife while he watched? Had I been hypnotized into thinking that those beautiful, boozy, ball grabbing canvasses were mine? Because they sure didn't feel like mine. And it didn't help that every time I scanned my memory for some kind of recollection of putting paint to canvas – some glimpse into their inception and progression – I came up with nothing.

At least I still remembered where I lived. The harsh white light bouncing off the whitewashed cinderblock of the hallway felt like it was calling out a reprimand for everything I'd done that night. I snorted at the profound oddness that watching Papa Scratch tuck into a living puppy was *not* the weirdest thing that happened to me this evening. I felt like it should have shocked me more, but I guess I'd seen it dozens of times. That's just the kind of guy he was. After all, he was the devil. Why didn't *that* shock me? In the fifteen years I'd known him, I don't ever remember thinking it was out of place. Had I always known he was the devil? *Yes*, a voice from the back of my brain shouted. And I had no problem with that? *No*, the voice shouted louder.

Okay.

I turned my key in the lock.

The place was a mess. I knew it would be. But tonight, something made me think it might be a little tidier. Like there'd be a woman's touch.

I dropped my jacket to the floor, tossed a half-finished canvas off the couch and flopped down. I looked at the canvas. It wasn't bad. In shades of purple, indigo and blue, a locomotive barreled toward the viewer out of the screaming mouth of a woman. Was this my work? *Yes*. I couldn't remember starting this at all. I must've been drunk. But I wasn't drunk now. So maybe I should try to finish it? If these canvasses actually came from me, then let's put that to the test.

I grabbed the palette and squeezed some tubes onto it, not even bothering to clean any of the brushes that were scattered around the coffee table. I propped the canvas up against the window.

I didn't know where to start, so I just started. I smeared a long line of midnight blue across the top left corner, and I saw a dusky twilight in it. Each time I daubed something new, I saw how I could immediately transform it into a part of the image, whole and perfect. I felt powerful. I felt true. I felt like an artist.

But I didn't feel in control. I didn't feel as if I were making any of the choices here. I was merely acting as an agent of randomness, sloshing paint here and there and letting a higher force decide what to do with it. I pressed on. I wanted to play along and see where this went.

As the first streaks of dawn came in through the window behind my canvas, I was done. It was as moving, as profound, as any of the pieces I had in the show tonight. But, like them, it didn't feel like it came from me. There was no connection.

I sank into the couch and tried to rationalize all of this as the mere workings of art, as the idea of the muse – some perfect, spiritual being who labors through my hands and my eyes to make works of stirring beauty. That must be it. That must be why I don't feel these canvasses are mine. Is there another explanation? *No*, the voice in my head whispered.

I'd stopped consciously thinking of the events of the night, but it was like they were playing on a video loop or something through my aching brain. Jesus fuck. I needed to clean up a bit. I needed to stop sticking my dick into stuff. Seriously.

There was a shuffle from the direction of the bedroom. I spun around and knocked the still wet canvas onto the carpet with a sticky sound.

A thin woman, wearing only a pair of my boxers, padded her way to the bathroom. She stopped at the door, suddenly seeing me.

"Oh, hi," she said, running a hand through her long dark hair. "You're home. Good. I'm just going to pee, then why don't you come to bed so I can suck your cock?" She grabbed my leather and wrapped it around her.

She was already in the bathroom before I could respond. I didn't get it – why was I so popular? Had it always been this way? *Yes*, the voice in the back of my brain shouted. Something didn't feel right about this. And didn't I just vow to stop sticking my dick in stuff? Well, maybe just one more. I'd play along just to see where it went. That wouldn't hurt, would it? *No*, the voice shouted.

Fourteen. That's what this whole night was like – some kind of adolescent wet dream, some schoolboy fantasy. Was this honestly my life now? *Yes*, the voice in the back of my brain thundered, making me duck and hunch my shoulders.

I didn't want to argue. I felt like a fourteen-year-old about to get his first touch of boob, that same feeling of giddy bubbling, that trembling at the back of the neck.

But it didn't feel particularly good.

I looked at the bulge of my gut under my Henley and my thin arms. I looked weak. I looked like I needed some kind of protection or armor. I looked for my leather and remembered what's-her-name had it. I wanted to wrap myself in its shiny, black safety for a minute. But no. She could have it. A wave of woozy sleep tugged at me. I'd had too much to drink. I just needed a second.

I thought of husbands and fathers, and of mothers and daughters. I thought of canvasses and blues, of highways and railway tracks. I thought of rest.

Without realizing it, I slipped slowly into the welcome arms of half-sleep, where visions of still-living puppies roamed free and sober along riversides, and of loving caresses and –

I don't know how long I'd been asleep. It was full light when boxers girl flopped on the couch and startled me out of my half-dream state.

"Wanna do some acid?" she asked innocently.

Yes, the voice in the back of my brain said.

7. RAMBLIN' ON MY MIND

I didn't feel anything at first, save the awkwardness of holding a small piece of paper under my tongue and the fear that I might accidentally swallow it. But she – I'd never gotten around to asking her name, though I must have known it once – was already on her feet and doing some kind of weird hippie dancing, gyrating her hips to music that wasn't there and waving her arms in front of her.

I raised a skeptical eyebrow.

She bent down, putting her hands on her knees and gently tossing her long, dark hair side to side. The globes of her breasts became a hypnotist's pendulum, and I was sure one of her nipples winked at me.

The walls of the room breathed in on me, closing around where I lay on the carpet. The girl was giggling, and each titter made the apartment hiccup, rattling the bottles strewn across the carpet. A school of mottled grouper swam by, slowed and gawked.

I needed some air.

It probably wasn't a good idea to walk out in the late December chill on my first acid trip – and me without my hat – but I was wholly convinced that it was a worse idea to stay in my cluttered apartment with a topless woman – who may or may not have had eyes in her nipples – dancing to unheard music, stretching and elongating, her dark hair coiling snake-like around her arms.

Just to be safe, I grabbed a blanket and threw it around me, watching as the crumbs it released skipped and danced to the corners of the room.

I was lost for an eternity in intense, purple concentration trying to get down the three flights of stairs, but the razor-sharp air brought me back to myself. I took a deep breath of it, wanting its ice to purify me, but all it did was make me cough and sputter.

Alright, I was getting too caught up in my own head. I knew that. I needed to be around people. I needed that basic human need of not looking like a lunatic to take the edge off the drug. I pulled my blanket tight around me and turned the corner to a main street, but every place seemed to be looming over me and smiling. And not very nicely.

I dodged around another corner, down another street, and tiptoed up to the first place that wasn't grinning.

I pulled open the door, nearly dropping my blanket in the process. Inside, it was dark. I was surprised to find this kind of place here, in the great flat expanse of the middle of the country. This place – all raw wood, old leather and wrought iron – had none of the dryness, none of the pragmatism of the black-miniskirt-clad sports bars I'd seen so much of in this city. Had it always been here? Or was it some new hipster venture? It looked old. If it weren't in some nondescript urban storefront with plate glass front windows, I would have said it had been here forever, since before the city, since before even the tribes had traveled and hunted across this land, since before human eyes had gazed in horror on this vast and sprawling continent. But that might've been the acid talking. The deep wood planks held together by nipple-warm, two-inch rivets, adorned with beautifully pointless door knockers, and the huge reliefs of crawfish against the lurid, teasingly sexual red brick walls looked like something from my paintings, which I still wasn't sure were mine.

Hey now! I ducked – the voice came from nowhere. And then more – *Hey now! I-ko, I-ko, un-day.* Oh. Okay. It was just the music. Crisis averted. *Jock-a-mo fee-no ai na-né, jock-a-mo fee na-né.*

The bartendress with rivets across her breasts greeted me. No. That didn't seem right. Her barely-there top was riveted along the edge. The metal glistened in the bar lights, reflecting candy-colored sparkles to my wide eyes.

"And what are you here for?" she challenged me.

"What?" I raised an eyebrow in what I could only guess was her direction.

"I said – what can I get for you?"

I didn't know. "I – I don't know."

"Lucky bastard."

I must have stood there for longer than was socially appropriate, judging by the quizzical look on her face.

"Or something else? It's just that Lucky Bastard vodka is the most popular around here. Thought you might enjoy it." She went back to drying a glass on a towel.

I looked at the bottles behind the bar and, even in my thrumming state, was able to locate the Lucky Bastard. The pinup redhead that adorned the bottle sat on an upturned horseshoe, pulling up her frilly yellow dress to reveal a length of black stocking.

Then she looked at me.

The vodka label girl lifted her chin and winked at me in a papery kind of way. Then she pulled her arm out of her frilly yellow dress, coyly, first one, then the other. She raised her eyes to mine as she pulled down the front. As the dress came down, all I saw was the clear liquor behind it.

"No," I said, perhaps a little too forcefully. "Can I get a papa scratch?"

I looked up to grab another glimpse of my coquettish, vodka-label temptress, but saw only the mirror. I saw myself, but something was off. The edges of my reflection didn't match the surroundings, like I'd been cut out, paper-doll like, and pasted here haphazardly. And behind me there were dogs.

They must have been five feet at the shoulder, three of them – one white, one black, one brown. They were snarling, with bared teeth dripping onto the dark, raw wood of the floor.

I spun around. And of course the hounds weren't there. That's how these things always play out, right? But in the far corner of the place, at a table against the glass that faced the street, were three people – a pale man with no teeth, a black-haired woman and a black man with a tilted black hat. I was achingly close to remembering where I knew them from, but when I tried to focus on them, the pinks and greens that washed out my eyes obscured not only them, but also any memories I tried to reach for.

I wanted to go home. But I wouldn't have been alone. Not that my boxers girl was bad or anything, but she just made me feel so … *lonely*. And what was the point of being lonely if you didn't even get the peace of being alone?

I pictured a house. A home. With people in it. People I wanted around. They were faceless, but hyper-etched in acid-induced detail. A wife and child. A home.

That was it. I'd give up painting, find a day job and maybe even sign up for an online dating service. Okay, maybe not that last one. Fifteen years ago, I'd chosen perfection of art over perfection of life. Time to redress that imbalance. Starting today. I looked up at the vodka bottle pin-up for validation. She winked at me again.

Okay, starting tomorrow.

The riveted bartendress plopped a drink in front of me. I supposed it was the rum and anise I ordered, but was made a little uneasy by the mint green and cotton candy pink that glowed from it in radiating waves. Something told me not to touch it, let alone drink it. It was a voice – no, a warning bell – a cascading warning bell that reverberated through my now vast and paper-thin skull.

The bell sank into its own reverberations until it became a trumpet. A clarion call above the jazzy counterpoint behind it. A blue line, snaking under and between the transparent ether of the ordinary world to enter my being, not through the ears, but through the skin itself.

I looked for where it came from, expecting something more transcendent, more alive than an mp3 player connected to a sound system. I expected a band, a band out of time, derby-hatted, antique and sepia. But that wasn't what I saw.

Along the back wall of the restaurant, there was indeed a band, in matching red uniforms with yellow hats, all playing as if they were damned to by some unholy tyrant. But dead, all of them. Their skeletal eye sockets stared emptily at me from iridescent skulls, some of them with jaws slacking into skull smiles. And still the music played.

A woman in the middle of the band, dressed in the same red with the same fleshless face with her long-ago rotted away breasts still poking teasingly under her dress, turned to me and beckoned. She swayed her protruding pelvis provocatively under the thin cloth of her dress. I wanted to play along and see where this went. *Yes*, the voice in the back of my brain said.

Leaving my drink to swirl pink and green inside itself, I walked to the stage, to the skeleton band and to my bony partner. She smiled – as if a skull ever did anything *but* smile. Then the music changed. It became somber, funereal. I was picked up by some of the members of the band and laid gently in a shining, black coffin. My skeletal dancer blew me a kiss and slammed the lid shut.

I could still hear the music, but it had lost its solemnity and become jovial. It had become a fanfare of horns lazily falling behind the beat of crashing cymbals. It sounded like a New Orleans funeral. My shoulders banged and bumped against the crimson satin lining. I beamed uncontrollably in the blackness. It felt somehow sacred to be stripped of responsibility for everyone and everything. Just to be picked up and taken away.

The bending of the blues was dancing and swaying with what was best and oldest in me, and it drew me along, leading me to an overwhelming question –

They put me down and the coffin echoed on a hard surface. Everything was silent for a long time. I didn't want to open the lid or get out. I wanted the safety – the *sanctity* – of my coffin. But. Where was I? Why had the music stopped?

Timidly, I pushed the lid of the coffin. It swung open with little force. The sky above me was red. I sat up, and I saw an empty landscape, all hard angles, illuminated in shades of red, crimson and scarlet. In the distance were the crumbling buildings that stood testament to what must have once been a great city. The low hanging clouds were underlit orange as if by a distant fire. The air smelled of charred meat and rotten eggs.

I stood up and felt both weightless and heavy, as if trying to run underwater. I'd stopped blaming the drug for what I was seeing. Using some kind of higher faculty, some kind of mode of thinking outside of and above rational thought, I stopped questioning. I knew whatever I saw was truth. I knew every aspect of it was the naked, holy truth. This was how things *actually* were and not the cave-wall shadows and desert-thirsty mirages of what I'd called, up to this moment in my life, the *real world*.

There was a wildness in seeing the truth, but that wildness kept a beatific calm center amid the turbid swirling of rending illusion. I felt good.

I looked good, too. I felt at least two inches taller and way more muscular than I'd ever seen myself. My leather was on, and it squeaked and groaned against me.

Gazing across the red-streaked mountains under the red sky, I saw Papa Scratch walking toward me. But this wasn't the Papa Scratch I'd known. I don't know how I recognized him. His old-fashioned suit and his hat were gone, and he walked naked, his skin the deep red of raw meat left out too long. Around his neck was a string of animal skulls, and the part of his face not covered by his huge, black, tangled beard was painted as a skull. He wore a top hat with a pure white feather stuck in the band. As he walked up to me, he was twirling a long, foot-thick tail that came to a conical point.

"Woody, my man," he smiled as he puffed on a long cigarillo. "I didn't expect to find you here. Something I can do you for?"

"So, this is where you live?" I ventured. It was lame, but I needed to start somewhere.

He looked at me quizzically, as much as I could tell from behind his painted skull. "I live in a lot of places, pal o' mine. This is one of 'em."

"You look different."

"Aw heck, man. You don't wear the same clothes every day, do you? Sure you always see me in my favorite suit. But that don't mean it's the only one I have."

Papa Scratch sat down in an antique-looking chair of leather and wood. There was now an office set in that barren, red landscape.

"You look so much at home here. I'd be damned if I had to spend too much time here."

Papa Scratch smiled. "Yeah, yeah you'd be damned." He picked up a drink that hadn't been there and took a sip. I could smell the spiced rum and anise. "But what makes you think you ain't damned right now, Wood? All of you people are damned."

I was inclined to agree with him. But I wasn't going to let on.

"That's a bit of a pessimistic thing to say." I leaned against the giant oak desk and raised an eyebrow.

Papa Scratch sat back in his chair and it groaned, not like leather groans, not like wood groans, but like the groans of the dying.

"It's quite simple, my man," he continued, holding his cigarillo between his tongue and top teeth. "You all damn yourselves. You all damn yourselves by failing yourselves and by failing in your relations with other people. By failing to be what's best and oldest in you when anyone else is around. Alone, all y'all are saints. Alone, all y'all are perfect, y'all do what y'all do without judgment, without angst.

"But, heck, once you throw other people into the mix – well, now there's trouble. Already you're up in your own heads about status, about reputation, about face, about just being *cool*. You're worried about offending whoever happens to be around you, or else you're worried about not offending them enough. So you sin. You sin by compromising the best and oldest parts of yourselves, and for what? To get a reaction. That's it. Just a reaction. For good or for ill. Do all y'all care about that shit so much?"

"Maybe," I said, recognizing how close he was to my own truth but hoping it wasn't quite as universal as he made it sound. "But what about those people who *like* to be around other people? Who feel most themselves when they're around others?"

"People who *like* to be around other people? What, like extraverts? They're damned worse than most. They actually *crave* the corruption of their own souls. They *want* the besmirchment. They're all up on themselves thinking they're feeding their souls, gaining energy, vampirically, from others. But they're all just running from the true sanctity of solitude, the holiness of just staying home."

"You sound disappointed. I thought you'd be happy for all those damned souls. You get them at that point, don't you? For your collection or whatever it is?"

"Disappointed? Yes, I am. I truly am. I wish all y'all could be good and true, whole and unbroken. It's not like I get off on tempting all y'all from the light and the way."

"That's not how I heard it. What about getting back at, you know –" I pointed to the sky.

"Aw, heck. I'm here to tell you right now, once and for all, the biographers got that all wrong. It ain't like that. I've actually never even met the Big Guy. It's not like we're some kind of diametrically opposed forces. We just got different hometowns."

"So God exists then?" I asked, thinking I'd caught him out, though not knowing how that would do me any good.

"No. Yes. Well. Not in any way you could comprehend."

"Kind of a glib answer."

"Why does it matter to you? It's not like it would change a single thing you did in your day-to-day existence. Would it, Woody, my man?"

I shrugged. "It might. If I knew for sure He was real."

Papa Scratch snapped forward and put his hands on the desk. "Well, ain't that just it?! Of course it would change things if you knew for *sure* He was real. That's the thing. You're supposed to have faith. Just like George Michael said. You're supposed to do good because of the *possibility* of the existence of God. If you knew for sure, you'd just be avoiding punishment."

"And where do you fit in?"

"Me? Man, I provide a service. People's lives is messy. All that random bumping around, never sure where they're going to end up. I tidy all that up. I make it whole. I make it make sense." He leaned back, and the chair groaned like the souls of the damned again. "You see, there's only one thing people ever really sell their soul for – to determine the course their own life will take. You'd think it would be more complicated, but that's it. They just want – and I personally feel they are *entitled* – to choose the course their lives take. Fame, power, money – these are all expedients to that self-determination."

"And you just do this out of the goodness of your own heart, do you?"

Papa Scratch chuckled. "Hey, man – I've got to eat and live, too, know what I'm saying? Of course there's a price. But it only costs them the blessed uncertainties, the little, random accidents that created the life they had. The life, I might add, that they're trying to get away from. Everybody wins. That's all I ever wanted, you dig? I just want to have everybody be real cool with everything. I just want all y'all to be *happy*."

"How's that going for you? How's the business going of robbing people of the – what did you call them? the blessed uncertainties? – that made them who they are?"

"Hey, now. Hey, now. No one's robbing anyone. It's just payment for services rendered. I find people think it's a small price to pay to have a beautiful, intentionally-designed life. And, since you asked, business is booming, man. I've never been so busy. I guess there are just so many people feeling like they're being forced toward a destiny, a pre-ordained life that they didn't choose – so they come to li'l ol' me. I just trade randomness for intent. You can't beat it as a business model."

He threw his thick tail behind him and pulled out something – how? from where? – blue and glowing that I felt was precious to me and so at odds with the hellish red of this landscape. The way it pulsed, the way it glowed so cool and blue and perfect made me want it. It felt like it was a part of me, an integral, lost part that had been calling to me, screaming to be reunited. I needed it. I needed it now.

I quickly gauged how easy it would be to just snatch it from Papa Scratch's hand. Not easy. And too dangerous. I'd have to play it cool while the torn half of my soul called out for its missing piece. But I could do it. I could play the devil's game as well the devil himself.

Couldn't I?

I needed to get him talking. "Is that what that weird little glowing blue thing is? Someone's blessed uncertainties?"

"Yep. This particular one is from a German woman who thought she'd made a mistake by not taking over the family farm. She blamed herself for her father working himself into a debilitating stroke, and blamed herself even more for how taking care of the man wore her mother down to raw-bone frailty. She made a deal with me. It was quite a treat. I so rarely get to visit Germany. Beautiful country out there. I've actually found –"

"What? You made a deal with someone to do something good? Something noble?"

"Yeah, of course. You don't get it yet, do you, my man? It's not about me. Damn, do I so wish it was, but it ain't. People get to choose what they want – they get to choose how they want their life stories altered and how they'll determine the course of them. I just deliver the goods."

"So how did it turn out? The German woman? She must have been happy about doing the right thing."

A slow grin spread across Papa Scratch's face. "No, man. No, she didn't like it at all. Heck, would *you* like being knee-deep in hog shit six days a week? She resented her parents – and that was truly the shame of it. She'd loved them so much when she'd thought she'd abandoned them. Now, having to put up with them telling her she's shoveling the shit wrong? She hated every split second of it. Truly a shame. It really is." He hung his head, still grinning. "Anyway, she found out somehow that we had made a deal to get her into this new life of hers – aw heck, I may have *told* her – and she wanted out."

"And? Is there a thirty-day return policy for peoples' altered life stories?"

Papa Scratch looked at me and smiled, this time genuinely, I thought.

A phone rang. As suddenly as the office set and drink had appeared, there was now an old-fashioned phone on the desk, as well.

"Yes?" Papa Scratch said into the receiver. "Sure. Capital. First rate. Yes, that'll do nicely, my boy. We were actually just talking about her." He turned to me. "You'll get a chance to see firsthand. She's here."

"What do you mean 'here'?" I turned to my left and a saw a stocky, blonde woman in hip waders and overalls. She didn't seem to notice me.

Papa Scratch had changed himself again. He was back in his old-fashioned suit and hat, and his long fingers. His skin had lost the red and was now his more familiar deep brown. His beard was gone and his face was unpainted. I couldn't see his long, penis-like tail anymore. Thankfully.

"Please," the woman said, in what sounded like English to me. "I need it to go back to the way it was. I would rather love them in my guilt than despise them with a clear conscience."

Papa Scratch steepled his long fingers and leaned back in the groaning chair. "But Greta, sweetheart – we had a deal. You wouldn't go back on your word, would you?"

The woman was silent for a long time. "Please," she said, almost inaudibly.

Papa Scratch sat forward and put his hands on the desk. "Let me get this straight – spell this out for old Papa Scratch. Are you telling me you would like out of our deal? And are you telling me that you're making this decision of your own free will?"

The woman nodded, looking down at the caked animal excrement that covered her clothes.

Papa Scratch lost his grin, and his face darkened. "I am truly sorry to hear that," he said, shaking his head. "I'm afraid I can't give you back what you had." He reached into his pocket and pulled out the glowing blue ball of light. He wafted it under his nose, as if sniffing the bouquet of a fine wine, licked it once, then swallowed it whole with a look of cat-like satisfaction. "It's gone."

Greta just stared at him. I couldn't tell if the blankness of her face showed rage or just an inability to understand what just happened. I watched her lower lip start to quiver.

Papa Scratch picked up the phone and said only one word. "Now."

And then a single, high, clarion note, sepia-toned, bent and blue – with all the lonesomeness of a train whistle – broke over the dust and the rock. It was everywhere – it permeated the hellish landscape with its high, lonely sound. And then it was right behind me.

I spun around, coming face-to-face with the large man in the black hat – the one Papa Scratch had been arguing with at my art show, the one I thought had been a six-foot hound – blowing into the harmonica he cupped in his hands.

"Greta, this is my associate, Mr. Blue," Papa Scratch muttered, waving his hand as if to shoo away a troublesome insect. "Mr. Blue will be helping me to harvest your living soul today."

Mr. Blue grinned, but his eyes were unmoved. It was a grin of only the mouth, showing what looked like too many teeth. I felt suddenly sick, like a candle had guttered out somewhere in the part of me where hope used to live.

Then the drums started. Slowly at first, and impossibly low – more felt than heard. But now increasing, both in speed and tone. Ra-DUM da-dum. Ra-DUM da-dum.

I heard a long, whispered exhale over the thunder of the drums and looked down. A man – was it a man? an animal? – with ashen white skin and no teeth was squatting in the red dust, snapping his head from side to side like a bird of prey.

Greta kept staring at Papa Scratch with her icy glare of hate, but he only smiled at her. "And this is Mr. Pale. If there's anything left of you when Mr. Blue is done, Mr. Pale will get to play with it." He furrowed his brow. "Mr. Pale takes his games *very* seriously."

A tear carved a path down the dirt of Greta's cheek. As I watched it fall, gently-lined, female hands rested softly on her shoulders.

Papa Scratch smiled as Greta turned around to face the new woman. "And this, Greta, sweetheart, is my favorite little witch. This is Ms. Fallen. That's *ms.,* mind you, not *miss*. Keep that clear. You don't want to make her angry. You know what I'm saying?"

Ms. Fallen brushed raven dark hair from her shoulders and pulled off her ivory scarf. She wrapped it around

Greta's neck, pulled her close and reached a finger out to Greta's forehead. What was that smell? It was sweet and nutty, with an unpleasant, rotten note somewhere in it. Ms. Fallen traced a shape on Greta's forehead, leaned in and kissed her gently on the mouth with moving lips.

Mr. Blue wailed another mournful note on his harmonica. Greta wept heavingly. The assorted figures on that dusty, red plain of hell all took on a funereal air and bowed their heads.

I didn't join them. I kept my eyes high. As much as I didn't want to, I *needed* to see what happened next.

Ms. Fallen pressed the first two fingers of each hand together and gently kissed the tips with closed eyes. She stepped away from the sobbing Greta.

Mr. Blue slipped his harmonica into his pocket and moved in, towering over the crying woman. He reached out a paw-like hand and, with a stretching and tearing of flesh that sounded like two overfilled balloons being rubbed together, slipped his entire arm into Greta's mouth. Her eyes went wide. I saw Mr. Blue reach down the woman's throat, and I saw Greta's lips distend over the padded shoulder of his suit. His tongue jutted out of the side of his mouth in concentration.

Mr. Blue smiled, seemingly finding what he was groping for in the bowels of the wide-eyed woman. He pulled his arm out and the body that had been Greta crumpled and fell to the red earth like so much discarded laundry. There was no substance left to her, only clothes and skin and hair.

But her eyes still moved. They flicked frantically, bleared with tears, scanning her small field of vision for anything that could mean salvation.

That's when Mr. Pale started his game.

He pounced over the fallen Greta-skin, his toothless smile directly in her face. Then he danced away, and she searched for him with panicked eyes. He leapt onto what used to be her back, and it made a sloshing sound on the empty skin sack. Greta gurgled. Mr. Pale danced away.

I turned, but I couldn't block Mr. Pale's rasping laugh or Greta's throatless glugging from my ears.

As I looked back, Mr. Pale grew bored with his ghastly peek-a-boo. He opened his gaping jaw and swallowed Greta's hollow remains whole.

I thought I heard her scream. But that could have been me. Then there was only silence. The drums had stopped.

When I opened my eyes – when did I close them? – the trio was gone and Papa Scratch had taken on his red-skinned, full-bearded, skull-faced, cock-tailed form again. He was tossing another – the same? – ball of blue light.

"Is that from another one of your victims?" I coughed. Watching the unholy demise of the German woman had made me bold.

"Yep. Yours, actually."

Thoughts whirred and clicked into place. In half a breath of that dusty air, everything made sense. That was why my life wallowed in the gutter. The devil had my real life. He'd taken all the accrued mistakes, wonderful and tragic, that had made up my life. My soul. It made sense. My life was crap because it was designed to be – *he'd* designed it to be.

Well, it was time to start cowboying up and stop letting others decide who I was and how I lived.

No the voice shouted in the back of my brain.

"Shut up," I shouted back.

Papa Scratch leaned forward again against the desk. "That's right, that's right. Of course you wouldn't remember." He leaned back. "You gave it to me, Wood, my man. You traded it for that perfect little life you're living right now. A simple exchange of randomness for design." He took another long swig of his anise and rum.

I panicked. I lunged, and I grabbed at the tiny, precious blue ball of everything that had made me who I was.

And I missed. By quite a wide margin.

I overbalanced and fell splayed on the cold, rocky ground of hell. Papa Scratch stood up and a few sticky drops of his drink fell on my prostrate body. His face looked somber as the grave.

"Oh, come on, Wood. That wasn't *right*. We had a deal. You gave this to me fair and square, and I gave you exactly what you wanted. A custom-designed life of your choosing. Everything you asked for – fame, talent, easy pussy. Randomness for intent."

"I want it back," I said not getting up, not even lifting my face out of the freezing, red dust. It didn't matter what the thing was. I'd decided I was going to take it from him. I was done being passive. I was done playing along to see how things turned out. I was just going to take it. "I changed my mind. Whatever it was – whatever messy, unintentional life I had – I want it back."

Papa Scratch smiled. "That, pal o' mine, is *exactly* what I wanted to hear. Are you saying you'd like to renege on our little deal, my man?"

"Yes. I'm out. We're done here."

"It's about flamin' time! Y'all don't usually take this long to weasel out. You may have set a new record, Wood. Yeesh – I've been hanging around for *hours* waiting for this. I have thrown every awful situation I could think of at you that fits the parameters of what you asked for, man, and you're only just now caving? Heck! I've had the damn hounds on my back all pissed 'cause this is taking so long." His face darkened and looked at me from the side of his eyes. "You're not some kind of ancient enemy of my kind sent here to slay me, are you?"

"What? No. Just let me out of the deal." Without lifting my head, I tried the last thing I could think of. "Please," I said as straight as I could and thought of Greta. I turned my face up to look at Papa Scratch, coughing on my passivity.

He looked genuinely mournful. His shoulders were slumped, and the cigarillo drooped from the downward-pointing corners of his mouth. "Well, then I'm sorry it has to be this way, my man. But a deal's a deal. Only one thing to do now." He turned his eyes to the red streaked sky and started speaking. Chanting. It was like the language I heard him speak to the pet shop owner, but this time it was harder, more stressed, with more hard, brutal sounds peppered through it. It was a violent language that reeked of bloodlust.

I stood up. I didn't know what was coming, but I knew I wanted to be on my feet when it did.

It started as a slow, steady pulse. The beat of a drum. Or a heartbeat. It may have been my own. Ra-DUM da-dum. Ra-DUM da-dum. Throbbing at first, then pounding. Ra-DUM da-dum. Ra-DUM da-dum. Soon it sounded loud enough to split the sky.

I wanted to run, but I didn't know where. The sound of drums was everywhere. What was there to run from? The pounding continued, shaking the giant, finger-like outcroppings of crumbling buildings and raising the dust from the baked earth.

A fierce wind blew gusts of the red dust into my face, and I closed my eyes against it. When I opened them, I saw the grotesque trio. Mr. Blue with his hat cocked arrogantly, Ms. Fallen with her black hair falling over her staring eyes, and Mr. Pale with his white body bent and twisted against the ground.

From somewhere in my memory, the words of the brassy singer in the blue dress came to me, as if a prayer from the lips of holiness. *The wind is hummin' through the churchbells, and the sky is turnin' pale. Seem like every time I turn to go, there a hellhound on my trail.*

It didn't help. The curved form of Ms. Fallen slithered up to me.

She reached out to me with her finger, and I smelled the sweet rottenness of her pungent oil. She traced an indecipherable symbol on my forehead. I couldn't move. I felt held by invisible hands. I felt as if my body had revolted against the commands my frantic brain was giving it, and it had sided with the ghastly woman, unwilling to bend to me.

Ms. Fallen stepped aside. I couldn't move my head to watch. I only saw the empty red dust that ringed the distant, finger-like ruin of rock in the distance.

But I heard the note.

I heard the lonesome, train-whistle note from Mr. Blue's harmonica, the same death knell note as for poor Greta. The sound reverberated in me, and something inside my chest, something good and pure and noble, shriveled and retreated down into the dark corners of my innards.

There was a scoffing, coughing snicker from somewhere, and I was afraid.

And there was something else under that refined, diamond-hard fear. I heard a pounding as familiar as my own pulse, but infinitely older. Infinitely more powerful. It solidified me. It rooted me. It made me ready for what I needed to do.

Whatever that was.

Mr. Blue palmed his instrument and took a step toward me, rolling up the sleeve of his jacket. Without planning to, I flailed at him, grabbing at what I could.

And I connected.

Something filled my hand that hadn't been there a second ago.

Mr. Blue looked *pissed.*

I looked down at my hands. Metal. Vibrating. It was the harmonica. The death knell.

I saw red murder in the giant man's dark eyes. But the pulsing drove me on. I put the instrument to my lips and blew. It hummed low with my breath, and I tasted dust and old gumbo.

And then nothing happened. Literally nothing.

Mr. Blue stopped his venomous trudge toward me. Mr. Pale stopped his head cocking dance. The wind stopped flapping Ms. Fallen's silk scarf.

Oh.

I shouldn't have done that.

I ran. I didn't know where to, I didn't know if it would do any good, but I ran. I ran for longer than I had lived, until the soles of my feet became red with the plain, and my antique lungs filled with dust and dry blood.

But then help. People. Normal human beings in this hell. Three of them. Women. As I approached them, I recognized them – the tiny Mrs. Prendergast, the macramé haired singer in the blue dress and acid-boxers girl.

I stopped. I felt less than saved.

I felt a vibration in my hand, looked again at Mr. Blue's harmonica. I had nothing left to lose. I blew into it tentatively and watched the women.

Their clothes slipped from them like rain off hot skin, as did mine. That was not the effect I was going for.

I took a few steps backwards, but all three of them covered the distance between us in a breath and were reaching out to me, clawing and scratching. And my flesh reached out to them against my will. I hardened, not from arousal but from pure chemical reaction to their naked, craving desire.

As their fingers dug into me, I wanted to slip this skin. I wanted my too weary flesh to melt so whatever was left of me could escape to … anywhere.

And then my skin and flesh did just that. Under their nails, all that covered my skeleton was rent and torn away with no more pain than tearing off an old bandage. My bones – with what I called *me* still in them – scampered away across the dust of that place.

Amid the red dust, my eyeless sockets saw more red. It was the red dress of my skeletal dance partner, who danced me into Papa Scratch's hell. Her bones barely filled out the cloth. She beckoned to me.

I had no muscles left to resist. My bare bones carried me into her arms and we danced. We danced until the red sky darkened and the screams of night howled. We danced until daybreak. We danced close, and I could feel without nerves the jabbing of bone against bone. I could hear without ears the grinding down of what was left of me, finer and finer, until I could no longer dance. My legs had been ground down to dust.

But she stayed by me. She rocked me as close as she'd danced with me, and what remained of my bones crumbled and powdered, mixing with the red dust of that place.

I wanted to weep, but I had no eyes. I wanted to laugh, but I had no mouth.

A gentle breeze scattered the pile of what was left of me across the plain and out of my own self-awareness. There was only peace. There was only calm.

I saw a young girl drawing a rainbow. I saw a grease-streaked old man pushing a shopping cart. I saw a husband and wife walking along a beach.

Then I saw nothing.

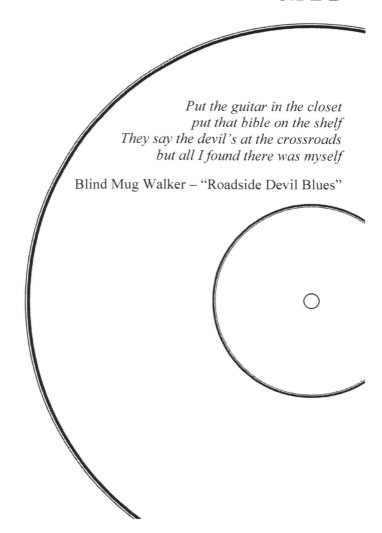

SIDE B

Put the guitar in the closet
put that bible on the shelf
They say the devil's at the crossroads
but all I found there was myself

Blind Mug Walker – "Roadside Devil Blues"

INTERLUDE

Sarah Osborne had never once poked children with knitting needles like they said.

With her knees on the hard wood, Sarah clasped her hands and took in a chill breath of the early March air, which hadn't yet let go of winter, but she didn't get the chance to pray.

John Baker and Ezekiel Strange threw open the door of her tiny house, and harsh wind swirled snow across her newly-cleaned floors. Sarah jumped to her feet, and there was a tightening in her gut and in her loins. She could hear demonic wings beating at her window, but that may have been the sound of her own frightened heart.

It was the fear on the faces of these two strong, young farm husbands that truly terrified Sarah. If they were this afraid of her, then perhaps she *was* the witch of Salem. She pushed against the feeling at her fundament, hoping there was some magic there – be it devilish or Christian – that could protect her, that she could force out against Goodman Baker and Goodman Strange. She pushed, but all she felt was a warm wetness in her skirts.

Goodman Baker grabbed her and fumbled with her clothes. Sarah whimpered. She thought he had intent to defile her there on the floor of her husband's house, but he only reached his thick hand into the pocket of Sarah's apron and pulled out what looked like an old, scratched bone. Maybe the ankle bone of a sow.

When Reverend Parrish came in, clunking his boots across the floorboards, he looked with contempt at the bone Goodman Baker held out as if it were something coughed up from the offal of the lowliest of God's creatures. He looked at Sarah, and his face became grave.

Sarah did not weep, nor did she speak as they took her on the hog-smelling cart to Boston. She only stared. She stared at Goodman Baker, who drove the cart, and she stared at Goodman Strange, whose job it was to guard the accused woman with a dull scythe, the only implement he could find as a weapon against an accused witch. She hoped – no, she *prayed*, but she didn't know to whom anymore – that her stares would shake their faith and they would ... what? Let her go? Dump her in the woods and leave her for dead? She was dead already. If the reverend believed she was a witch, then she would surely be hanged. The trial in Boston was mere Puritan theater.

As the days passed, it wasn't the jail Sarah minded. It wasn't the rats or the human stench of excrement and misery. It wasn't the strangely carved bone they'd tossed in after her, a constant reminder of her false accusation. It was the time. It was the awful endless hours. At home, there had always been more than enough to fill the hours of a long, working day. But here, in the Boston jail, she was alone for nights that turned to days and days that turned back to nights, alone with her sureness of oncoming death and her uncertainty about her prospects in heaven. If she were truly a witch, there would be only damnation.

It was in the ancient, unending hours of solitude where Sarah saw the face of terror. Then her visitor came.

At first, she thought he was just a shadow, for his dark skin and dark clothes barely made an impression on her jail-wearied eyes. But when he held up his hand, and she saw the long, willowish fingers, she knew he was of blood and of flesh.

"Hiya, sweetheart," he smiled as she hugged herself. "Well, ain't you in a bit of a ... situation."

She knew there was something wrong with this, that she should be afraid, that this was ungodly. But she had been so alone in here with only herself, with only her fears. For weeks? Months? She had no idea. So she listened to the dark-skinned man.

"There's something you're looking for, ain't there, darling? Something you want to know? You can tell old Papa Scratch." He smiled in a way that made Sarah's eyes want to turn away in revulsion, and yet she stared.

"Yes," she ventured meekly.

Papa Scratch stepped a step toward her and held up his long, nobbled fingers. "Well?" he shrugged. "What's on your mind, baby? There a question you got?"

There was. She could feel it burning in her gut. No, lower than her gut. She felt its flame in her shameful organs, urging her to hate and to revenge with more raw power than it had led her to either of her husbands' beds. The one question.

Why?

Why was she here? Why was she here in this jail, in this seething, filthy city, away from her home and her children?

Why?

"Why?" she whispered.

"What's that, baby?" Papa Scratch said cupping his long fingers around his ear. "I didn't quite hear you."

"Why?!" Sarah screamed from the depths of that fire that burned in her fundament. Her scream bleated against the stone walls of the jail and seemed to shake them in rollicking agreement, seemed to roil the fetid earth at her feet, bubbling it up until the small, marked bone rolled dirty in front of her.

Papa Scratch smiled. "I got an answer for that one, sweetheart. That one's easy. But I ain't going to just tell you. Heck, you'd never believe me, you know what I'm saying? This one – this one you got to see for yourself."

Sarah knew what the man was talking about. But she didn't want to know. Anything she had, anything she could give, she would happily part with for a glimpse at the machinations that brought her here as an accused witch in a fetid Boston jail. She even would've offered the man her body. But what he was asking was different. He was asking her to take clear and decisive action. To *do* something, not just passively receive his desire. He was asking her to, of her own free will, take part in the very devilish ways she had sworn she was innocent of.

"You'll just need to bury that little trinket in the floor here," Papa Scratch explained. He looked around the cell for a moment, not finding what he was searching for. "I guess we can forgo the whole crossroads thing, seeing as how … we're, well, where we are." He smiled again, a little too broadly. "We'll just say you're at a *crossroads* in your life. That'll satisfy the requirement."

Sarah didn't know she was going to do it until she gathered her skirts, squatted down and dug through the foul besmirchment that made up the floor. When the bone was buried, she felt no different. And the man was gone. She sobbed softly.

It started with a pinprick in her throat. Then more – an odd, pricking numbness at the back of her neck. She opened her mouth, ready to pray, but her voice had become hoarse and scratching, the sound of dried, snapping wood, or the call of a great black bird.

Sarah covered her mouth with her hand, but she kept cawing, hoarse and raven-like. She looked down. Flowing from her skirts were a hundred thousand deep red wasps, each as large as her palm, smoldering in the dirty air.

She screamed – she tried to scream – but heard only a raven call.

With ravenous mandibles, the wasps ate at her clothes, stripping her bare. Then they bit at her skin and her hair and her flesh.

Sarah Osborne could now no longer distinguish between terror and agony. They had both become the same wave washing over her, had become only the feeling of skin exposed to a January morning as she drew water. The bitterness of fear and the acidity of pain had detached themselves from her, becoming too heavy to be a part of her failing body. Split from these, she was able to watch what was happening to her.

She was able to watch as the wasps bit and ripped away, in tiny yet effective bites, everything that Sarah had been and regurgitated a blue-black oil that slicked onto her bones and transformed her. She felt light. She felt powerful.

Her sharp eyes darted around the room, not seeing what they had seen before, not the human misery of incarceration, but just the human stain. She knew this was not a place she should be, so she shook her black feathers with a snap, spread her wings and flew out of the barred window into the skies above Boston city.

She knew where she needed to go. She may have known all along that her ideas about her malefactor were true. But she needed to see with her own black raven eyes. She needed to see it was her own family who had plotted her accusation and her death.

As Sarah – no, not Sarah anymore, she was a nameless, fallen woman now – flew over the fields outside Salem village, she saw the man. Husband to her husband's sister. He was standing in a field he didn't own as if it belonged to him. He noticed a raven alight on a nearby fence, and he smiled smugly, comfortable and relaxed in the knowledge that his plan had been a success. He'd expanded his lands threefold, and at such a small expense. And better, he was doing God's work. If there were witches in Salem, they would be flushed out by his whipping up rhetoric.

The raven cocked its head at him. As he looked into its black, liquid eyes, he wondered, only for a moment, if the creature knew, could even comprehend, the plan he had just seen to fruition.

It could. The raven that had been Sarah Osborne now knew that she had been innocent, that she had always been one of God's children, that she had not strayed, even unknowingly, from good nor from truth. But she didn't want to know. The hatred that burned in her for this man, for what he had done to the woman who had been Sarah Osborne, made her want to turn from God and from goodness and into true congress with the unholy forces, to exact revenge on the man and his family.

She felt betrayed. Not betrayed by this man, not betrayed by her God, but betrayed by her own true self. She was good. She was holy. And now she wasn't. This grain of truth she had seen in the fields of Salem village had left her betrayed by herself. She wanted to *unknow* it. She wanted to go back, even if that meant to a stinking jail cell awaiting the noose. Her God would have been waiting for her on the other side of death.

He would not be waiting now.

She screamed, but again heard only the raven call. She needed to undo this. She needed to break the deal. And so she flew, she flew back over the fields and the forests to the filthy city. Her sharp eyes found the jail, and she flew back again through the barred window. With her beak, with her talons, she rent and tore the human-stained ground, searching for the buried bone.

It wasn't there. But the long-fingered man had returned.

"Sweetheart, sweetheart. Baby," Papa Scratch said. "It ain't there. You can't go back on a deal like this."

From somewhere – was it his broad mouth? – the smoking red wasps swarmed again, pulling apart the raven feathers, snapping open and filling Sarah's bones, and regurgitating human flesh and skin and viscera and hair. Soon, painfully, Sarah Osborne stood again eye-to-eye with the long-fingered man.

"I cannot know the truth," she whispered, still hoarse and cawing. "Take it back. I cannot. For I fear I may turn away from God if it is not plucked from my memory. Let us break this bargain, I beg of you on all that is holy."

Papa Scratch grinned and let out a series of slow, low chuckles. "Look, babe. I wish I could help you. I really, honestly do. But I don't make the rules. I gave you what you wanted and didn't even ask for anything in return."

"But – my eternal soul. It shall burn."

Papa Scratch flicked his tongue across his top teeth several times in quick succession. "Yeah, well, that was an unforeseen bonus."

Sarah held Papa Scratch's eyes. She could feel tears well up in them as she began untying her bodice, but she didn't look away. As she exposed her breasts to the fetid air of the jail, it was he who broke eye contact.

"Hey now, hey now. I'm flattered about the offer and everything, but you don't mean it. I mean, come on. You're crying. Even *I* have my limits." He smiled. "Besides, it's not like it would change anything. That wasn't what you thought, was it?"

She didn't cover herself. She felt if she moved at all, if she even breathed, the tears and wails that were threatening to overcome her would subsume her entirely. But that thought alone was enough to break her resolve, enough to let pour forth the misery of the malefactions. She shrieked and pulled at her hair, weeping and mixing the salt of her tears with the mud and excrement of the floor.

Papa Scratch lost his grin and his face fell. "Whoa, whoa, hey. Don't get all worked up about it. There's nothing *I* can do. But it's not like you don't have options here."

Sarah thought she could hear the baying of hounds over her own sobbing.

"Look. I can always use some help … collecting certain debts from people who aren't too willing to pay them. You could help me with that. It can be a slog sometimes. But it's got to be better than an eternity of damnation, right?"

Sarah didn't remember ever making any signal of assent, but she knew she had agreed, and she knew somehow that her eternal soul was now in service to the long-fingered man. From the black ground beneath her, came a man pale as a morning frost. He grinned a toothless grin at her and opened his mouth wide. As the pale man's lips wrapped around the entirety of her body like soft sheets, she felt at peace. Sarah felt as if she were merely slipping into her own bed after a long day's work. She felt calm.

But she did not feel God's breath anymore.

The thing that had once been Sarah Osborne's soul still very much looked like her. She had the same mild, handsome face, the same ample breasts, and the same curve of the hips. But her virtuous brown hair had been turned a ravenish blue-black. It was this figure who stood at the back of the crowd on the tenth day of May when the empty vessel of Sarah Osborne's body was publicly hanged for witchcraft. This new being, who shared the dead woman's face, felt nothing. As the gallows dropped, she felt at peace. She felt as if she had fallen a long way from a holy pedestal, only to find the world better, richer and more exquisitely varied down here on the ground. She was thankful to her master for that, and she served him well.

Together with Pale, the woman who had been Sarah Osborne – who now was only known as Fallen – collected the souls of those unwilling to pay the debts of their deals. But she had none of Pale's cruelty. None of his iciness. She was calm in her work. She understood her victims, and she understood why they wanted what they wanted. She blessed each one with a kiss, a benediction against their sufferings. Then she drew a horned mark on their foreheads in a pungent oil, whispered a prayer over them, and watched, stony faced, as her associates ripped their living souls from their bodies.

8. STOP BREAKIN' DOWN BLUES

The carpet scratched at my left cheek and something soft caressed my right. My eyes fluttered open, but I saw nothing. Then a vague, elongated pink and black shape started slowly moving toward me, coming directly at my face. There was a pungent smell in the air and a dull, airy thump. Somewhere not far away a harmonica wailed hard on the blues.

"Sh, sh," she whispered in my ear.

I stood up with a start.

The woman wearing only my boxers – and now my leather around her shoulders – knelt on the floor, a bottle of essential oil in her hand and a pair of beaten up bongos at her feet. I half -expected her to hand-tear the meat from me.

"Jesus fuck!" I screamed, far too loudly for the little apartment and the distance between us.

She pulled back and looked genuinely hurt. "You – you just looked like you were having a really intense trip – I was casting a protection spell over you."

"Spell? What spell?"

"A protection spell."

"I don't care what kind of spell it was! Why in the name of fuck would you think I wanted a spell cast on me? Jesus!"

"You looked troubled. I wanted to soothe you." She took a step toward me and tried to sexify her voice. "Like I promised I would last night with a *different* kind of magic."

It was probably meant to be seductive, but all I saw were staring, bulging eyes, yellow and distended from rot. Her smooth skin took on a green pallor, and maggots chewed their way out of her cheeks. The room reeked of rotten meat and old metal.

"Get out," I whispered.

"What? But, babe."

"Get out," I said even more quietly. I'd had enough. I'd had enough of spells and magic and being anointed with oils and devils and deals. I'd had enough of women I didn't know or care for constantly being around me, being in my house, being in my head and denuding my bones of skin and flesh.

I was done.

I grabbed her by the wrist. "Get out!" I shouted, and it reverberated off the windows. I jerked my leather jacket off her shoulders, and she dropped the bottle of essential oil.

She covered her breasts with her arms and thumped to the bedroom in full petulant teenager act. "Rude!" she shouted loud enough for me to hear but not loud enough that it would seem aggressive.

I pulled at my beard and tried to take stock.

Why had I never questioned my friendship with Papa Scratch? In the fifteen years I'd known him, why hadn't I ever delved into how truly, headshakingly strange it was that I hung out in bars with the devil? It was time to start asking some questions.

I heard a kind of exasperated, huffing sound made of indignant female breath and the apartment door slam.

Then everything shifted half a step out of time and quickly settled back.

It was an almost imperceptible shift, slight yet profound. It was the feeling of someone else in a room thought empty. It was the sudden oddness of seeing a familiar hallway reflected in a mirror. It was a crack in the foundation of my memory. Things were, in that moment, different than they had been a split second before. But somehow, impossibly, they had always been that way.

I had memories that weren't mine. I had memories that contradicted each other. A wedding and a bride in white with a red bouquet – my wedding, my bride – on the same day as my graduate art show. I remembered a baby that was and wasn't mine, and I remembered canvasses that were and weren't mine.

Nausea burrowed its way into my lungs and stomach. It took me a second before I realized its source in the spilled bottle of patchouli on my carpet. The whole apartment now smelled like the inside of a vintage Volkswagen microbus.

Great.

I needed some air. I tried to read the clock on the wall, but the numbers and angles refused to coalesce into any meaningful information. I looked out the window – the sun was getting low. Afternoon in December. I'd find a place to have a drink to steady my nerves. I'd find Papa Scratch. I had some questions for him about all of this. Yeah. Everything would be fine.

As I walked, I felt like an *artist*. This was good. This is the life I wanted. I felt like me.

And only for a second did I doubt what I meant by *me*.

I don't know how long I wandered with my coat collar to the cold amid the twinkling of Christmas decorations. I ducked into a shopping mall to warm up at one point and was thrown crushingly into a flux of random, last-minute-shopping motion that pulled and pounded at the cracked edges of my drug-wearied brain. I left by the nearest exit.

I came across a vast and unpleasantly cheerful Christmas display on the front lawn of an old brick house that lit the street up. Happy, happy elves and red-cheeked Santas smiled and waved at passersby, no matter what scoffs and raised eyebrows they got from their audience in return. The image of wholesomeness the scene projected was in stark contrast to all the witches and devil deals I still had banging around in my aching brain. How could this be Christmas? Carolers were singing *Silent Night*, and here I was thinking I had a hellhound on my trail. I shook my head and looked up. The bluing of the sky told me I must've walked until early evening.

I needed a drink.

I ducked into the nearest place – plate glass front and heavy, riveted wood inside. Had I been here before? It didn't matter. It was a relief to be away from the throng of Christmas shoppers. I hadn't realized how nervous they made me until I'd made my escape.

I sat down at the bar and ordered a cheap, domestic beer in a bottle. The bartender made a face and glanced at his watch, but brought the drink promptly enough.

The place was nearly empty. The news of the day scrolled silently across a TV along the back wall. A pair of old women sat in the corner rustling through purchases. An old-timer, who looked like he'd become at one with his barstool, was planted a few places down from me. A young couple made young couple eyes at each other by the window, probably trying to get as many minutes together as possible before going home to their families for Christmas frolics. Or whatever people do.

And there was me. "How about this weather, hm?" I cast out in the direction of the bartender and the old-timer/barstool hybrid. The old guy grunted, obviously well accustomed to deflecting casual conversation. The bartender ignored me and dried a glass.

I didn't want to be alone. The acid was wearing off, and I needed some comfort. I didn't want to spend the rest of the night inside my own head. I half-regretted kicking that topless woman out of my apartment. Then I remembered the bongos.

I pulled out my phone looking for someone to call. Papa Scratch was my first choice of course, but I remembered he didn't have a phone. Why hadn't that ever struck me as odd before? Oh well. So, who's next?

I thought of the singer in the blue dress from the hotel bar – she of the copper, macramé, spiraling hair – and ignored the whole acid-fueled, flesh-rending incident. Did I even have her number? It didn't matter. I couldn't remember her name. If I ever knew it.

Scrolling past nine Cayleys, six Kaileys, three Caylieghs, a dozen Emmas and an Ingrid – who were these people? – I found the number for Braden Prendergast. I wasn't going to be alone tonight. I decided that I hadn't given that whole situation a fair shake. After all, he'd only wanted to do good by his wife. And Melissa – well, she had a genuine thing for me, even if it only was because I knew my way around a paintbrush. I'd decided they were good kids. I'd almost forgotten that she was part of the unholy trio who'd stripped me to my bones. Yeah. I'd give Braden a call and set something up for tonight. My frayed nerves felt a little better at the thought.

He was hushed and hurried when he answered. "Yes?"

"Hi – Braden? It's Wood Sweeney."

"Yes, I know. What can I do you for, Wood?"

"How are you? I just thought, if you're not doing anything tonight, that we could get together again. Give it another try. If Melissa's up to it, of course."

"Oh," he said, surprised. "I surely did not expect to hear you say that. Melissa will be thrilled. She's talked about very little else – you must have made quite the impression on my little lady." His voice became hushed again, and serious. "But look, Wood. We'd love to see you again, we surely would. But it's just that we're at my in-laws for dinner tonight. Can we make it maybe sometime in the new year? You know – build up the anticipation a little."

Well this wasn't any good. I was starting to see why I disliked Braden after our first encounter. I wasn't looking for company in January. I was looking to stave off being alone *tonight*. "Come on, Braden. The offer might expire by then. Ditch your dinner and let's get a hotel somewhere." I tried to sound as seductive as I possibly could while talking to another man about boning his wife.

There was a short silence on the line. "Wood? Are you asking me to spirit my wife away from her parents' house on Christmas Eve to have sex with a total stranger?"

Christmas Eve? Since when was today Christmas Eve? If it was, then that was exactly what I was asking. "Are you up for it?"

"Merry Christmas, Wood," he said and hung up.

Well goddamn. Not wanting to be alone, I'd gone through my list of "friends" and found that it consisted of a guy who thought he was the devil (and had no phone), far too many unremembered female acquaintances than I was comfortable with and a willing-cuckold husband that I'd met once. Was that it? How did I get to forty years old and have that as my list of friends? I supposed for a moment that I must've alienated, by intent or by neglect, everyone who'd ever tried to make a connection with me. It was a sobering thought. Too sobering.

I ordered another drink. Something more medicinal. Again, the bartender pulled a sour face and looked at his watch. But he brought me the scotch.

I scanned the room – the man/barstool creature was still there, but everyone else had left. All I had to look at was the muted news channel on the television. I thought I recognized the face on the screen from way back in my past. She'd aged. But there was still the pretty dignity in the angles of her face, now gently lined with years and worry. Her black hair, streaked subtly with white, was pulled back, and her eyes barely hid their tears.

The words scrolled across the bottom of the screen. *Fentanyl Deaths Continue to Soar.* I idly pulled at my beard as I took them in without noticing. I was looking at the pained, struggling face of the woman being interviewed. *Laura Blumquist*, the screen said. That made a connection.

Of course! Laura. From grad school. We had a thing. We were in love. And I –

I'd pushed aside that thought for so many years that it had become second nature to ignore it. But I was alone on Christmas Eve with my shabby list of two friends. I couldn't sink any lower. I was ready to say it. I was ready to admit it to myself.

"I left her when I found out she was pregnant with my child," I whispered. Something flushed out of me – a cold, black feeling that I'd been holding on to, a poison I'd gotten so used to that it became part of me. Now, my blood ejected all of it, purifying itself in the mere act of confession.

I coughed something up in a fit of hacking and nearly fell off my stool.

Laura Blumquist. She could've been the love of my life. But I chose perfection of art over perfection of life. Idiot. Any fool knows that perfection in either is impossible.

She was being interviewed about her daughter, another fentanyl fatality. When I put together the pregnant girlfriend I'd left fifteen or sixteen years ago with the high-school-aged dead daughter that she was being interviewed about now, the room became perfectly still and roared away. My vision became a cone pointed only at my hand on the bar, and all I could see were the lines and the hairs on the back of it. My daughter was dead. I wasn't there.

I'd only been twenty-four or twenty-five, so maybe I had no idea about how these things worked, but I honestly could have seen myself settling down with Laura Blumquist. Raising our child. What stopped me? Painting? And where had that gotten me? It felt hollow now. The whole idea of living as an artist now felt like it had been broken open, scraped out and forced back together with sloppy brutality. It all felt meaningless.

"Laura," I whispered and cleared my throat. My eyes scratched at themselves, and my chest was cold and tight. I'd never met our daughter. I never would.

I couldn't fathom going back to that apartment, still reeking of patchouli and black magic, so I ordered another drink.

I held up my glass and rattled the ice in it, trying to catch the bartender's attention. I didn't want to speak. I knew if I opened my mouth, I would scream out all the grief and rage until there was nothing left of me. If there was anything left of me now.

I rattled the ice again, the bartender turned, pulled his now familiar disapproving face and looked again at his watch. "Come on, man. I've got to get out of here sometime. Go home to your family. It's Christmas Eve."

Something tired and shaking inside of me gave way, and everything else came rushing out of the gap it left. "Why the fuck does everyone keep telling me what day it is?!"

The bartender took a step forward and loomed over me, putting a glass down hard on the bar. "That's it, pal," he said calmly. "You're out of here."

I stood up. I honestly thought that I had every intention of just putting on my leather and walking out. When I didn't, it was like I was watching myself from outside, and wincing at every new escalation.

"I'm out of here?" I smiled and turned, making it look like I was going to leave. But as I went, I picked up the pint glass he'd put down on the bar and let it slip from my fingers onto the tile of the floor. It shattered satisfyingly. "Oops."

The bartender balled up his rag and threw it to the side. He marched around, flipped up the door in the counter and came out from behind the bar.

The half-man/half-barstool had backed off his beer in the commotion. In one long, graceful move I picked up his half-full pint and hurled it across the room. Its contents sprayed and splattered the freshly cleaned tables, chairs and floor, and it was spiraling toward the plate glass window at the front of the bar.

In the microseconds I had to look around, I saw a figure outside in a blue police uniform.

Oh.

I shouldn't have done that.

A pounding in my pulse tensed me, and I shot my hands into my pockets. I pulled out Mr. Blue's harmonica without even being surprised that it was there. What – did I think I was going to play a jaunty little tune and my act of wanton vandalism would be dismissed?

I blew a few notes, out and in, and the air sucked out of the room. The dim light swirled together with the dark blue outside and everything was midnight quiet.

And the pint glass hadn't made impact yet.

I looked toward the front window, and saw, suspended over a table for two, the glass with its contents captured in long globules of floating liquid.

I looked at the harmonica. Okay. I had a magic mouth harp that could stop time.

Glancing back to the bartender – his face was frozen in a not-at-all-pleased expression – I tried to wrap my head around the situation. This wasn't real, right? I didn't really just stop time.

The bartender slowly jutted his head forward. No. I hadn't stopped time. But I did slow it down. The glass and the airborne beer were crawling along to their plate glass destination.

I should have left right then.

But it was just too weird. I wanted to play along and see where this went. I smiled as I stuck my finger into the suspended beer and tasted it. Hang on – was the glass moving faster?

I put the harmonica back to my lips and played around for the same combination of notes. Here? No, that made the glass move even faster. This one? Nope. Faster still.

I was still blowing notes as the pint glass smithereened against the plate glass at the front of the pub. The crash resounded for a few seconds.

For a long time, everyone was still. I thought for a moment they were still magic-mouth-harp-time-slowed.

But then motion. The figure in blue was walking from the front door toward me. She was tall and definitely dressed in a police uniform. Crap.

"Ethan?" she said to the bartender. "Do we have a situation here?"

She looked familiar to me, but I couldn't place her.

"Constable Santiago," bartender Ethan said. "Your timing, as usual, is impeccable. This gentleman decided he preferred to throw shit around than go home to his family for Christmas."

She turned to me. "Do we have a problem here, sir?"

The rage had drained out of me. I was hollow. I didn't want to be here anymore. "No, no problem." I turned to the bartender. "Look, I'm sorry. Stressful time of year and everything. I'll clean it up. I'll pay for any damages."

"It may not be as simple as that, sir," Constable Santiago interrupted. "Ethan here may decide to press charges, in which case there will be the formality of an arrest and booking. Ethan?" She turned to him.

Ethan just stared for a moment. Would I be spending my Christmas Eve in a police station? I thought of my daughter. I thought of Laura. I didn't give a damn anymore what happened to me.

"Nah, forget it," Ethan said, relaxing his shoulders and turning back to the bar. "Merry Christmas."

Constable Santiago looked back and forth between the two of us a few times. "Alright, sir," she said to me. "Do you have a place to go?"

I thought of my witchery-stained apartment. "Yes," I muttered, feeling like a nine-year-old in trouble with a teacher. "My apartment's just down the block."

"Would you like me to escort you?"

Oh, God. The thought of it made me want to weep. I blew one last time into the magic harmonica, hoping I could stop time and sneak out. The squeaky note only made her wince. Oh, well. "No. No, thank you," I said. "That's a kind offer. But I think I'd like to just take the walk alone." I tried a weak smile. "It might be good for me."

Constable Santiago looked skeptical, but walked me to the front door and let me go. As I left, I glanced up at the television for one more look at the life I'd left behind. They'd moved on. It was a news story about the garish Christmas display that I'd seen earlier in front of the brick house and how heartwarming it was. I walked out into the newly fallen and still falling snow.

I didn't go far. I wasn't going home. I don't think I could ever call that apartment home again, if it had ever felt like home. The wave of adrenaline that had come over me by smashing the glass had waned and ebbed away. I was left with a pervasive, solid-feeling exhaustion, which tried muscularly to wrestle me into submission and sleep.

I'd just sit down for a while. Just for a minute. I needed to. I could barely lift a foot through the miniscule amounts of fluffy snow on the ground. Every step sapped my will. I would just rest for a second. That was all.

I shot a glance over my shoulder to see if Constable Santiago was following me. She wasn't, but I wasn't about to take the chance of having her stumble on me again. I ducked a ways down an alley and sat down on a tipped over plastic garbage can with my back against a cold brick wall. I would just rest for a minute. That was all.

I watched the large flakes of snow fall on the leather of my jacket, pause a moment, then melt away. It became hypnotic. I watched the snow fall on me slowly, and as each flake fell, it took longer for them to melt. I didn't feel the cold. I didn't feel anything except the heaviness in my limbs, in my eyes and in the whole of my being. I was a sad, middle-aged man slumped in an alley on Christmas Eve, slowly succumbing to the blanket of fresh snow.

I didn't feel myself fall asleep.

9. KIND HEARTED WOMAN BLUES

The light forced its way into my eyes slowly, in ever-widening cracks. A downy sensation of consciousness spread outward from my eyes, into my limbs, fingers and toes, and I felt warm. The feeling of being completely and fully used up, right down to my remaining thin wisps of soul had nearly wrestled me under. But it had now quit the more violent part of its assault, leaving me free to wake up, wiggle my toes and roll over in the soft, shampoo-and-lotion-smelling sheets.

But the fatigue hadn't let go its hold enough to allow me to grasp the significance of where I was, what I saw or what I smelled. I didn't even start to wonder why I was in this soft, feminine-scented bed, or how I'd gotten out of the alley and the snow. Under the exhaustion's still-loosening grip, I was only able to luxuriate in the utter perfection of the first seconds after waking naturally. But, as perfections do, it slid away from me down a long, icy ramp made of thinking and panic and worry.

Where was I? How did I get here? Why didn't I remember last night?

I pulled back the sheet, got out of the bed and looked around for some kind of clue. I wasn't naked – that was a good start. I still had my Henley and my boxers, but I didn't see my jeans or leather. I scanned the room. It was definitely a woman's. I didn't see any trace of masculinity here, just lotions and bedside reading and decorative pillows. There was a picture of a kid – a dark-haired girl with braces, smiling goofily at the camera.

And there were sounds from just outside the door.

I froze. My ears became hypersensitive and searched for more input. Dishes clanged. Something sizzled. I could smell bacon.

Cautiously, I opened the door, and the sounds and smells of breakfast washed over me. A woman in a bathrobe, her dark hair tied back, was standing at the stove with her back to me.

How much of last night did I not remember?

She looked absorbed in what she was doing, and I didn't want to startle her by just calling out or walking up behind her. But I also wasn't thrilled about standing in a stranger's hallway in my underwear. I tried shuffling my foot on the carpet, but she didn't hear it over the sizzling on the stove. I cleared my throat.

She spun around, looking at first alarmed, but her features soon shifting into a smile of recognition. "You're up. Hi." She clutched the spatula awkwardly.

Had we met? I had an impulse to shake her hand. She looked familiar, but I wasn't going to trust my recollections anymore. So instead, I went with the stammering-like-an-idiot plan.

"How did I –? Did we –?"

She looked surprised, and her expression quickly slid into scandalized offense. "What? No. No, I – I –" Stammering seemed to be contagious that morning. She gestured to the frayed couch pushed against a window, made up as a bed, the sheets and pillow obviously slept on.

I looked at her face. There was definitely something familiar about it, and it also looked like she'd been crying. Recently.

"I found you," she said, finding her words. "You were outside. It was cold. It was snowing. I didn't want to leave you, you could have –"

"Died?" I said, beating her to the word. "Would that have been so bad? You don't even know who I am. I could be an awful person."

"I know who you are, Wood." Her face became stern, and her eyes darkened. "And there's been too much death," she said with a fresh rasp in her voice.

"Laura," I whispered. Laura Blumquist, the could-have-been love of my life. I must have been farther gone than I thought if I didn't recognize her after that news report last night. My eyes unclouded, the kitchen dropped away and I saw only her. I might have wobbled a bit on weakened knees.

We looked at each other for a long time. We didn't speak. She turned her back when the sizzling of the bacon in the pan demanded her attention. But I didn't want to lose this moment – I couldn't let the spell of what had just happened between us be broken. That instant of perfect connection. If I let it slip, we would be back to small talk – the how-have-you-beens and the so-nice-to-see-yous. I needed to re-establish that manifest, solid kinship and not let it slip away.

"What was she like?"

I saw her shoulders start to twitch rhythmically in silent sobs. I crossed the distance between us and gingerly touched the top of her back. She turned into me and buried her head in my chest, wailing and weeping. I held her for what felt like fifteen years, but couldn't have been more than a minute judging by the eggs.

When she'd collected herself, she looked up at me, her eyes red and searching. "I'm sorry," she said and looked away. "I shouldn't have –"

"No," I interrupted. "*I* shouldn't have. I shouldn't have left. I should have been here. This whole time." I cast my eyes to the floor. "What was her name?"

"Makayla," Laura choked. "And she was a good kid. She really was. She had her problems, but —"

The sobbing overtook her again, but this time she busied herself with spooning scrambled eggs onto chipped plates. She brought our breakfasts to the table and sat down. I did the same at a chair that held my leather jacket and neatly folded jeans. We never made eye contact.

We ate our first few bites in silence. "This is good," I ventured, pointing to the food with my fork. We were into small talk.

"Thanks." She paused. "She needed a father." She still wasn't looking at me.

Okay, no more small talk. She was right, of course. Of course she needed a father. She needed *me*. And yet still some voice in the back of my brain demanded that I defend myself, that I justify my actions, that I say what I did was unequivocally for the best. A thousand excuses came to my head at once, and I took a sharp intake of breath, ready to start defending. But I didn't say anything. There was nothing to defend.

"Yes," was all I said.

Laura looked up at me, her eyes rimmed with tears. But it wasn't a look of reproach. It was a look of pity, a look of sorrow.

"Are you okay? I mean, I never told you about any of this," she said.

"I didn't deserve to know."

"Wood! She was your daughter. Of course you deserved to know what a great kid she was. I just couldn't … the way you left …"

"What if I married you?" I said, a plan formulating in dim corners of my brain as I spoke.

"What?" she said taken aback. She stood up and started clearing the dishes. "Wood, we barely know each other. It's been fifteen years."

I didn't know what she was talking about for a second. "No, not now. What if I *had* married you before our daughter –"

"Makayla."

"Makayla. What if I'd married you when we were twenty-five? What if I'd been there to protect her?"

"Wood, don't do this to yourself. Don't beat yourself up. Honestly? Yeah, it probably would have been different. But. No. There's nothing we can do now."

Again, I was confused. She wasn't following me. "No, you don't understand. I'm not talking in hypotheticals or conditionals." The ideas were coming fast now, popping perfectly-formed little heads into my brain. This could work. "What if I *actually* married you before Makayla was born? What if I could find a way back into that life? It would save her, wouldn't it?"

She sat down, and in her face I could see she knew how serious I was, that I wasn't just waving my fists in the air at cruel fate, damning the gods.

"How? You can't rewrite our life stories," she said, and her shoulders slumped.

I didn't know how far I could go with this. I didn't know how much I could tell her. She was right – we barely knew each other. Was I seriously going to tell her I was friends with the devil himself and that I could make a deal? That I could go back and right a decade-and-a-half-old wrong?

But it was still Laura. She was grayer, older, wearier – but it was still the woman I'd loved once. I could tell her anything. When I'd known her, she believed half a dozen things stranger than this before breakfast.

"I know a guy," I said timidly. "Well, not really a guy. He's the devil."

"Why? What does he do? He can't be as bad as all that."

"No, Laura." How was I going to sell this? "He's *actually* the devil. He calls himself Papa Scratch. He makes deals. He could get us what we want."

She was skeptical. And who wouldn't be? I'd gone too far. I'd lost her. Again.

"Put the pan back on the heat," I said. I had no idea if this was going to work the way I wanted it to. Or at all.

She titled her head in confusion, but got up and turned the burner back on.

I picked up my plate and dumped my half-eaten scrambled eggs onto the smoking pan.

"Wood! You'll burn them."

I looked into her eyes with mine wide and shook my head. "No, I won't. Watch."

I took her hand – as if I believed physical contact would stop her from being slowed. From the pocket of my leather, I grabbed the harmonica and blew into the third hole, then the second, then a draw and frantic waving of my harmonica-holding hand.

Nothing happened. But not in a good way. Time kept ticking its tyrannical beat.

I tried again to remember the combination I'd played in the bar. I blew into the second hole, slid up to the third hole, then drew in and wowed my hand.

The sizzling slowed to whalesong depths, and I watched the oil splatter slowly and arc its way painstakingly slowly to the stove.

I looked at Laura. She looked at me and smiled. At regular speed.

Without my willing it, time resumed, and the once meandering smoke from my unfinished eggs raced upward and wailed the smoke detector.

Laura passed me a magazine, and we both batted at the smoke until the deafening alarm slipped back into silence.

Quietly, we sat back down at the table. "You seem to have a phylactery," she said.

"I do?"

"The harmonica. I'm sure it's a phylactery – kind of like a good luck charm, but way more powerful than any rabbit's foot. It's kind of like a witch's familiar, only not an animal. Something inanimate"

"How do you know these things?"

"Wood, if you're going to go around telling people that you know the devil and stopping time with a magic harmonica, you're going to have to bone up on your mystical talisman lore." Her face darkened again. "It must have chosen you. It must want to be with you."

I thought of Mr. Blue and shuddered.

She leaned forward and put her elbows on the table. "Go on. You were telling me about how the devil is a good friend of yours."

So, I told her about Papa Scratch. I told her how we'd been friends for fifteen years – since I'd walked out – but how it wasn't until two days ago that I ever questioned his claim to be Satan. I told her about my acid-induced vision, about meeting the devil Papa Scratch in hell, about Greta the German farmer who'd reneged on her deal with him, about the tiny glowing ball of blue light. What did he say it was? The mistakes and accidents that made a true, real life. I told her how Papa Scratch showed me my own ball of blue light, how I asked him why he had it, and how he said something about a deal. I explained to her the events of the last few days – leaving out a few choice details about women, washrooms and puppies – she just nodded and listened. If I could get her on board, this might just work. I could make a deal with the devil to change my life story. To get my family back.

"The universe will right itself," she said as she made coffee. "I'm not saying I believe all this devil stuff, but I do know that life abhors a cosmic imbalance. If you try to make this deal to change everything, the universe will right itself. You can't change anything permanently. Things are meant to be a certain way. You never believed that." She took a sip of coffee with both hands cupped motheringly around the mug as if simultaneously absorbing its warmth and bestowing hers, exactly the way she used to. "I knew for sure that we'd be together very early on."

"You told me four dates in, if I recall. Bold move."

"Well, I guess I was wrong."

We looked at each other without focusing, both lost in the same thought. She wasn't wrong. We were meant to be married and be together.

"Your deal with the devil. It's already been made," she said, setting down her mug.

"What?" I thought about it. "Of course it has. Do you think that's why I've only started to question Papa Scratch in the last couple of days?"

She was wide-eyed now. "Yeah. And it's why you've suddenly become dissatisfied with this life of the artist you've had since we split – again only in the last few days. Why else would Papa Scratch have the blue light with all the accidental turns in your life? You made a deal with the devil for the life you have now – probably two days ago – and this is what you asked for."

"What?" No.

But.

Yes.

Of course it was. I didn't want to let her be right. I wanted to fight against the idea. But I forced myself to face the possibility that this was my devil-deal life. It made perfect sense. She was right. Papa Scratch had been telling me the truth on the barren, red plains of hell. I'd made a deal with the devil for the life I had now.

"But I don't know what you can do about it," she said, refilling our cups. "It's not like I'm an expert, but I don't think you get out of diabolical bargains easily."

No. You don't break a devil-deal easily. I'd seen that with Greta. But I had a plan. It came to me perfect and plump in all its details. Papa Scratch probably made it impossible for anyone to break his bargain. But I didn't need to break the bargain. I just needed the ball of blue light. I was sure of it. The blue light was the life I left behind – it was all the mistakes and accidents that made my true, real life – traded in for the too-perfectly designed husk of life I was living now. It was my *soul*.

Of course, it would be a little hairy getting the damn thing from Papa Scratch, but with a little luck I might just have a chance. All the pieces clicked into place. All that was left was finding him. And that was the easy part. I just needed to wait until sundown.

I explained everything to Laura. I'd need her help. In fact, she would be the one the whole thing rested on.

"We can do this. Seriously."

She looked at me. "You've changed. What happened to just wanting to see how things went? You're not the man I almost married."

"I'll take that as a compliment."

We didn't talk about the implications for her. We never mentioned that, if all of this were true and if the plan worked, she'd cease to exist. At least she as she was now. I felt like a coward for not being able to bring it up. But the muffling grief that covered her had lifted slightly, and it was like something old and good within her was beginning to flow forth again. Did she realize her life could blink out of existence? Or is that what she wanted? To be free from the suffering.

"Or we could just forget it all," I said and forced a smile. "Let's just get away. Forget Christmas this year. We could jet off to someplace sunny and tourist-drenched, wear botanical print shirts and cameras around our necks? Hell, maybe we'll even stay. I'll build a house by the beach –"

"*You'll* build a house?"

"Well, I'll get some help building a house by the beach, I'll paint, you'll garden – think of what you could grow! – and we'll be together again. Come on – go pack a bikini."

Laura held my eyes, and a I tried to make them sparkling enough to convince her. The corner of her mouth twitched, and, with the façade broken, she chortled halfheartedly into her cup. "God! How often did you use that line with me?

Let's just get in the car and drive to Mexico. How far could it be?" She locked her eyes on mine. "Maybe you haven't changed that much, Wood."

"Seriously. We could just leave. Put all of this behind us. I have some money. I think. I might. Let's forget it. It's a dumb plan. Let's just hop on a plane and see how it goes."

She stared at me with newly reddened eyes.

"No," she whispered. "If you can do this, do it. If there's a way to." She cleared her throat. "If there's a way to bring her back, I need you to do it."

I only nodded.

Silence, eyes on eyes and half smiles punctuated what was left of the years between us.

"Well," I ventured more cheerily than I wanted to. "I guess I should –"

"Should you?" She wasn't crying anymore.

I swallowed, but it did nothing to drown the pounding in my throat.

Maybe it was just that we were both at our absolute nadir, each of our souls scraping the hard bedrock of as-bad-as-it-can-get. She took me by the hand and led me to her bedroom.

We stood, fully clothed, on either side of the bed she'd saved my life in, just looking at each other. We were two people at the beginning of our fifth decades – a little worn, a little spread out – but I saw her as more beautiful than she'd been in the tight-bodied years of our mid-twenties. She was a woman. Strong and frail, flawed and perfect.

I held her until she fell into warm, afternoon sleep.

I lay awake and the air pulsed in time with me. I made up my mind. I would rewrite our life stories. I could give Makayla a second chance. At that moment, my life – my entire being – was secondary to setting things right. Whatever that meant.

The orange of the afternoon retreated to the oncoming blue. It was time to go. There would be no last-minute getaway to exotic beaches. There was a plan to put into action. There were lives to right. We put our coats on without speaking, but only exchanging that little language of old lovers, the brushing of hand against back, the moving of hair behind ear.

"Laura? If this works – you know what it means, right?"

She pulled her hair back, tied it and kissed me on the cheek again. "Ready to go?" she asked.

I traced the same route from the redbrick downtown out to the suburb's edge that Papa Scratch and I had taken after my show. Laura and I didn't speak. At one point I took her hand, or maybe she took mine. I couldn't tell. Our hands just folded naturally together.

Walking with such determination – such singularity of mission through the crowds of cars with families packed inside, off to whatever Christmas obligations they had – was all something I'd never felt before. Laura and I alone were blades of a single purpose cutting through the fat of the festivities. It was good. It was good to do this with her. It was good to just be with her.

It was dark by the time we got to the pet store, and the temperature had dropped. A shiver started in my belly and radiated outward. Would this really work? And if it did, did I want it to? I was standing beside the woman who I was convinced, once again, was the love of my life. And I was about to chuck that all in for a life I knew nothing about. I rode my hand along the small of Laura's back and wondered if she'd be there. Or if she'd be the same.

I rapped on the locked door of the pet store in an approximation of the same rhythm Papa Scratch used. It must've been close enough, because a little gnomish woman poked her head out. Her squinted eyes widened when she saw Laura and me instead of the devil she knew.

"Hi," Laura said with enough syrup to drown a short stack. "I'm *so* sorry to bother you, and especially on

Christmas, but, it's just that – oh! I'll just come out and say it. My niece *so* wants a puppy, and I thought my husband here got it, but he didn't – typical, right? – and I was just wondering if – I know that it's *Christmas* and all, but would it be possible to just take one puppy away with us? Honestly, I'll pay whatever price you're asking. Well, my husband will since this is all *so* completely his fault."

The gnomish woman dropped her defensive posture but stayed in the doorway blocking the entrance. She shook her head silently.

All right. Now it was my turn.

I dashed a look at Laura, and she nodded subtly. This was it. I pulled the harp from my jacket and blew – the second hole, sliding up to the third hole, then a draw and a wowing of my hands. I was sure that was what I did in the bar last night when I threw the glass.

Laura's face was locked with mine, and I could see the frantic anticipation in the lines around her eyes. But she didn't move. I slid through the partly opened door and hefted the statue-stiff, gnomish woman into the air, surprised at how light she was. I threaded a zip tie around her wrists and pulled gingerly. With her secured, I drew air through a high note on the harp and time ticked by at its normal pace again.

The gnomish woman spat out a few curses in her Ukrainian-sounding language.

Laura slipped in and behind me. "Are we really doing this?" she said breathlessly.

The adrenaline pounding its way through my body after stopping time so I could tie up a quite-possibly-not-human old lady pet shop owner hardened my muscles and slacked my nerves. I was powerful and calm. I kissed Laura hard on the mouth. My heart pounded in my ears and pulsed through me into Laura. I nodded. "We're doing this."

We looked at each other. We looked to the gnomish woman. We looked to the floor and the ceiling.

Laura broke the silence. "How long can he go between … you know?"

"Disemboweling puppies for nourishment?"

"Yeah. That."

"I have no idea. But, knowing him, I don't think we'll be here long.

The old woman had quieted down, but her slitted eyes still stared hatred at me. I couldn't look at her anymore.

"Tell me about Makayla," I said, mentally counting the ceiling tiles and pulling at my beard. "What was she like?"

"Mak?" Laura was wandering idly, running a finger along the glass cages and watching the puppies and kittens try to scratch and paw at it. "She was good. Stubborn. She was never satisfied. She refused to accept things the way they are. Always wanted to change them." She stopped walking and turned away from me. "I guess she was a lot like you."

"Laura – I –"

Something tapped a rhythm on the door. It was time. I shoved my hands into the pockets of my jacket, trying to coil myself into readiness, and I felt something warm. I pulled it out. It was that stupid goat coin Papa Scratch had given me after I'd saved him from that bloodlusted quarterback. He owed me a favor. One unrefusable favor is what he said. Maybe I should call that in? Ask him for the blue soul marble.

Yeah, right. I scoffed at myself from the back of my throat at the thought that this coin could make Papa Scratch do anything he didn't want to.

And anyway, it was too late. Laura was already opening the door.

"I'm *sorry*," she said in her honey sweet voice. We're closed for *Christmas*. But *thanks* for coming. Stop by again tomorrow."

She closed the door slowly, but, like I knew he would, Papa Scratch wrapped his long fingers around the cold metal of the door frame and forced it back open.

"Well, well, well," he laughed. "Looks like I've been caught out. Had to happen, I suppose. Had to happen. What are you – SPCA?" he smiled broadly. "I think we might be able to make a deal." He clicked his teeth together three times.

I grabbed Papa Scratch's arm with both hands and, with the momentum I'd generated lunging toward him, spun him into the pet store as Laura slammed the door and bolted it.

"Woody, my man? That you? Now what on God's green would you be doing in a place like this, my man?"

I didn't answer. I didn't need to. I'd got him talking. Laura had already slipped her hand into the side pocket of his jacket and pulled out the small ball of blue light. I could see its glow through her flesh, and I felt again uncontrollably drawn to it, as if it fulfilled a perfectly empty need in me.

"You want to know what I'm doing here?" I said finally. "Just getting a little something that belongs to me." Laura tossed me the glowing ball, I caught it and held it up for Papa Scratch to see.

"Oh no, man, no – say it ain't so! You did *not* just do that." He hung his head in his hands and shook it slowly. "This is not going to end well." He looked up at me and smiled. "For you, I mean." He said. "Everything ends well for me."

"You told me this was my life," I said holding out the ball of blue light. "You told me that this was all the random chance and mistakes I'd made to be the person I was. My soul. Well, I'm taking it back. All of it."

Papa Scratch chuckled and cast an open palm around the room. "You'll lose all of this, Woody, my man. The fame, the talent. And the pussy. You know you'll lose the pussy, right?"

My eyes shot involuntarily toward Laura. I regretted it.

Papa Scratch smiled even more broadly. "Oh ho ho! You don't *care* about the easy pussy anymore, is that right?" His smile dropped, and he lifted his chin high. "But you'll lose her, too, Wood. That woman standing over there is a part of this life. The life I designed for you. She won't be like this if you go back. She won't remember you like this, all brave and ruggedly manly. Seriously, man – think about what you're doing."

I looked at Laura again, this time intentionally. She only nodded. I could already see in her eyes the hope. I could see the grief and the elation and the sheer relief of this life being over. So it didn't matter what I was going back to. It only mattered that this woman, who I'd once loved, could be spared the pain of losing her only child to a meaningless death. I'd done some bad things, but this was the single, noble thing that I alone could do.

I looked at the ball of blue light in my hand swirl and pulse. I'd made up my mind, but the problem was how to make it manifest. I looked to Laura and raised an eyebrow.

She read my confusion and, without missing a beat, pointed a finger to her opened mouth and shrugged. Of course. These are all the mistakes I'd made to become who I had been. And everyone's got to swallow their mistakes.

Papa Scratch's eyes bulged as I moved the blue ball of light to my mouth, popped it in and swallowed it with a cartoon-like gulp.

I mouthed the words *I love you* to Laura. For a few seconds, the three of us just stared from one to the other, blinking and confused. And then I felt my body stretch, twist and expand along ancient, cosmic nerve patterns that reached from this suburban pet store in the great plains in the middle of the country all the way to the far ends of the universe and farther.

It hurt.

INTERLUDE

For Rodney Baraquin, going to the crossroads and making his deal was never a question of *if*, only of *when*. His father had been out to the crossroads – at least that's what Rodney's mother always said. The only two things Rodney knew about his father were the deal at the crossroads and the stories of the heartbreaking blues he played. Rodney knew about the finger bone with the strange carvings, and he knew that his father had traded his immortal soul for the power to blow out his suffering in the holy contours of the music. The way Rodney's mother told it, Rodney's father had, with some kind of mojo hand or black magic, used the beauty of his blues to slip the poor, innocent Miss Baraquin to sin, in her own parents' bed, and leave her a fallen woman with a boy child in her belly.

Rodney was seventeen now, and, after seeing the kinds of lovers his mother took to her bed, he was beginning to doubt that any black-magic musical talent would have been needed. He was beginning to doubt that his mother's time with her lovers was anything more than a business transaction.

Devil deals and music are not the kinds of things that tempt the holy Christian folk. But despite this – perhaps *because* of it – for as long as he could remember, Rodney wanted to be like his father. He wanted some skill, some ability that set him above the other boys around, set him above even the grown men. He wanted the power his father devil-dealed for – the power to entertain people, to make them happy, to wrench their sorrows from them in pure, transcendent blue notes. Rodney Baraquin had a burning desire for the wailing, bent sounds he'd heard in the sawdust-floored speakeasies and the streets of the big towns. He wanted to open himself up, take what he felt to be his soul, set a sputtering match to it and burn it into the blues.

But, of course, he didn't want to have to work too hard to do it.

When he was fourteen, Rodney swindled a skinny kid out of a dinged old harmonica in a crooked card game. Rodney knew the wimp wanted to call him out as a cheat and a thief. But Rodney had always been a big kid, and was already becoming a big man. The skinny kid slinked off, leaving Rodney to blow the first few tentative notes out of his new treasure.

They were squeaky, screechy notes. And Rodney couldn't figure out how to put even two of them together to make a melody. As the heat rose in the damp alley, he tried a few more times with the same results, until he just smashed the thing repeatedly against the bricks of the whorehouse's back wall with enough force to make his knuckles bleed.

But Rodney could still feel the unexposed and unburned blues within him. He needed a way to bring them out. He thought of his father. He thought about deals and devils. The trouble was, though crossroads were aplenty, human finger bones with the right rootwork scratchings weren't easy to come by. Only the toby maker would have what he needed. So, one night, when she was off administering the last rites to the last woman in the town to be born into slavery, Rodney broke in and sifted through her hanging chicken feet, her roots, her malodorous powders, her mummified animal phalluses. He couldn't find the bone he needed and left with only seventeen dollars he'd stolen after breaking open the woman's strongbox.

No, for what he needed he would have to go to New Orleans. And he'd already spent the seventeen dollars.

The night the rains started, the rains that would eventually cover the land and would be known as the Great Mississippi Flood, Rodney had been running a while with a gang of sharps. They were mean men with blackened teeth and blades under their shirts. It was September, and they huddled under a back-alley awning out of the rain. One of the men, a wiry guy with a snaggletooth and a scar under his left eye, had a harem of the lowest of streetwalkers, and they hadn't been able to turn any tricks in the deluge. He was cocaine-wired and mad. Rodney was scared, even though he must've weighed twice as much as the little man. This guy was a Mardi Gras firecracker, and you never knew how much of a fuse was left.

The gang had just held up the post office, and Rodney had been lookout. It was his eighteenth birthday. As the rain rattled like dropped marbles on the corrugated tin above them, the men split up the take.

"No, man. Not three ways even. Don't forget the kid."

"Fuck the kid," the wiry man said. "We didn't need no lookout in this rain. Ain't nobody out."

"Aw, hell. I guess you're right. Fine. Three ways even. Sorry, kid. Not tonight."

They'd promised him. They'd said he'd get a share of the cash, and all he had to do was to watch and make sure no one was looking. This was going to be his ticket to New Orleans. This was going to be his talisman. This was going to be his blues.

Growing up large, Rodney had learned, like a great ape, to hold his aggression back until the right moment. He'd learned to let a lot of things roll off his back until it was time for the upstart to learn a lesson. That night, in the gunfire clanging of the rain, Rodney forgot everything he'd learned.

He grabbed the wiry man by the throat and pummeled him, rapidfire, like a gymnasium speed bag. The man's blood splattered Rodney's face. The other two men in the gang stood up, but held their distance. Neither of them could match Rodney for sheer strength. Barely audible over the rapping of the rain and the dull sound of fist on face, the wiry man gurgled. When he felt the man go limp, Rodney dropped him into a faceless heap.

Blood was dripping into his open mouth, and Rodney was breathing hard. He sensed more than saw movement behind him and spun around. The other two guys in the gang were inching closer, their knives drawn.

Rodney was unarmed, but he knew where the wiry man kept the switchblade he used to threaten his girls. In a motion, Rodney stooped, pulled out the man's blade and waved it at the other two. He shouted something indecipherable. The men backed off.

Rodney knew he'd done some bad things. But killing a man was different. This crossed the line. This made him a real criminal, more than the petty thefts or occasional beatings ever could. And he was eighteen now. No leniency from the law anymore.

So Rodney ran. He didn't know where to run, so he just ran. For days, weeks, he skulked, he sneaked and he hid along the edge of town. Under porches, behind dumpsters, anywhere to get away from the endless, endless rain. And then, just before Christmas, Rodney found the graveyard. It was cold, but it was shelter. He didn't think anyone would look for him here. If anyone was looking for him at all. If anyone cared that he killed the wiry man. In his mind, he saw an image of the wiry man's whores rejoicing, and he smiled. Maybe he hadn't done such a bad thing, after all.

Rodney spent Christmas Eve in a crypt with the bones of some well-to-do white woman. He talked to her remains and sang her Christmas songs in a rough-hewn blues voice. It was never as good as he wanted it to be, but he had an uncomplaining audience.

That was the day one of the wiry man's stable of whores found him. She'd been looking for him. He'd set her free, and she wanted to repay him. So she did. She repaid him with her body on the cold damp floor of the crypt on Christmas morning.

In the months that came she brought him food and, when she could, money. She told him about what was going on in the town, about how they were still looking for him, but not very hard. The wiry man was a bad character, and the police weren't too broken up about having him gone. Rodney may not get a medal if he went back, but if he stayed away the authorities might be convinced to look the other way.

They became lovers, the ex-prostitute and the murderer on the lam. They met in the crypt, they ate, they laughed, they made love. Despite the relentless rain, the cold and damp, it was the happiest Rodney could remember being. He only rarely thought of the wiry man. He never thought of his mother. But he thought of his father often.

The blues still burned within him, calmed occasionally by his lover's touch, but still wanting to burst out of him in full flame. And Rodney still had no means and no talent to make it manifest. He knew he had to get his talisman, the marked bone and get it to the crossroads before anything could happen.

He never talked to his lover about this. He rarely talked to her about anything. He was intimidated by her. He knew how many men she'd had. He knew that he was just a mannish boy in her eyes. And so he came on tough, stony, perfect. Maybe that's why, Good Friday, she didn't come to meet him. The rains came strong. This was no earthly torrent – it must be retribution from a vengeful God or a torment from some mischievous devil. Rodney woke up that morning as rainwater sluiced into the crypt and into his sleeping mouth. He went outside and looked to the horizon.

All he saw was the rain, the rain falling and the rain fallen and the rain filling the gutters.

Because the levees on the river hadn't broken, the rains that lashed the towns on the riverside had nowhere to go. They bounced off the sodden ground and into the streets, into the buildings, into Rodney's crypt, and the levees trapped them. He was ankle deep in water as he walked out into the cemetery.

Something cold and sharp brushed by his ankle. He kicked at it, but found himself locked in its unshakable grip. He shifted his weight, ready to pull his leg free, and felt the same thing on his other ankle. He was trapped, and he panicked. He pulled at his leg without shifting it, but the strain overbalanced him, and he plunged into the cold, coffee-colored water, swallowing a throatful and sputtering.

Rodney felt the same icy fingers clutch at his arms and his throat, and he flailed wild-eyed and frantic. And then he saw the bones. As he writhed against his unseen restraints, Rodney knocked and smashed against bones floating on the filthy water. He thrashed and pitched, sending the unburied remains dancing in devilish patterns around him. His head knocked hard against a skull, and his eyes closed. No, his eyes were open, but he was under the murky water. Rodney opened his mouth to scream, inhaling a mouthful of the mud along with something hard.

And then he was released. He was free. The bony fingers that held him were gone.

He didn't know it at first. He stayed half-submerged and suffocating under the surface. There was a calm about being here. A sense of peace. He'd moved past the panic of breathlessness to the utter bliss, the near-sexual ecstasy of oxygen starvation. The world turned deep red and warm, and the stars in front of his eyes smiled at him. This was what life was about. Water. Warm. Wellness. Hope. Warm.

No. No, none of these. Cold. And death. This was wrong.

Something inside Rodney snapped open, and, like a carnival lightshow chemical reaction, burned him back into where he was. He was in the flooded graveyard, banging against bones. And he was drowning.

Rodney kicked with the warm pools that were all that remained of his legs. He grabbed with the thin spiders that had been his hands. Slowly, with echoed crackling and burning, the oceanic, slow-motion sounds of underwater snapped into hardness and coldness, and air flamed in his lungs.

He coughed pink, blood-splattered water for as long as he could remember. And then he was whole again. Whole, wet and *cold.* Rodney gasped and sputtered, but something stayed with him. He felt a hardness in his mouth, and he spat it out with a hot hatred.

He looked at the thing in his hand. It was a bone. A small bone. A *human* bone. Maybe from the foot or the hand. But it had been defiled. Sacrileged. It had strange, unintelligible marks all over it.

Rodney looked closer. The markings were kind of like the symbols and scratchings he'd seen at the toby maker's place, but harder, more angular, more *violent*.

He knew what it was. Maybe he'd known what it was before he even looked at it. It was the holy, ungodly talisman that would seal his deal and bring him release from the torment of the unexpressed blues still in him.

Amid the bones of the dead rising from their graves in the corruption of flood waters, amid the panic of the town for high ground, amid his own near-death, Rodney Baraquin smiled.

He moved slowly, standing up in the dirty water and marching out of the graveyard to the road out of town. He was deliberate, and yet every motion felt completely outside of his control. He was pure motive, a pure cutting edge unto his purpose, hard and sharp and unyielding.

Rodney Baraquin, the talisman gripped hard in his giant fist, was, for the first time since his screaming, squealing birth, utterly calm and utterly himself.

It was the first crossroads he could find. It would do. He tore at the wet earth with his fingers, and it squelched and collapsed in on itself. Frantic, he cast around for anything he could find to help, snapped a branch off a nearby tree and shimmied it into the muddy ground. He kept the hole open long enough to drop the rootwork talisman into, and he watched the mud and water take back the groove he'd made.

"Rodney Baraquin," a voice said behind him.

Rodney spun around and cocked his fists, ready to pummel whoever had interrupted him in his most holy of tasks. He didn't recognize the man in the suit and hat. But he knew.

"You him?" Rodney grunted.

"Rodney, my man. You has to have a little more politesse than that when you're dealing with a gentleman of my refined character." The man wiggled his long, birdlike fingers and took a step toward Rodney. "What makes you think I wouldn't just smite you right here?"

Rodney gulped. "I – I'm sorry, sir. I didn't – I didn't mean no offense."

"Aw heck, man. I'm just jiving with you. No reason to get all worked up. I ain't smited no one in near a hundred years. Come on."

Rodney stared.

"Well?" The long-fingered man continued. "This is the point where you tell me what you want. Where you tell me all about how life's been so unjust to you, and how you just want to redress the balance. Isn't that it? Some wrong step you took long ago, and you just want to see how things might have turned out if you did it differently. Or maybe you just want to know the truth? Maybe you just want to know *why* your life took the twists and turns that it did. Hm? Any of that sound familiar?"

Rodney knew what he wanted. Of course he did. It was all he'd ever wanted.

"The blues. I want to play the blues."

Papa Scratch shrugged and spread his long fingers questioningly. "That's it? It's easy enough, but not a very sexy wish." He spat his toothpick into the mud. "Why?"

The desire had been in residence in Rodney for so long, he'd lost the ability to see it. Why did he care so much for the one thing he cared about?

A man without a face walked across Rodney's mind. A faceless man with a trumpet is his hands, bending sweet and hot blues from the bell.

"My father," Rodney said.

"Yes? What about him?"

"I – I want to be like him. I want to be strong."

Papa Scratch walked a slow circle around Rodney. "Looks like you's more than a touch strong already there, big fella."

"No. I want to be strong inside. I want a way to get the rage out. Music, sir. That's the way."

Papa Scratch stopped when he came to face Rodney again. "No deal."

Rodney let out a whimper. "What? Why not? I did all's I was supposed to do."

Papa Scratch pulled out a new toothpick from somewhere in his mouth with his tongue. "Meh. I don't know. You just don't strike me as the artist type. I've known me some artists, and you ain't like them."

Rodney felt the rage build that he only ever barely kept in check. His fist whipped out and hammered Papa Scratch hard on the nose.

Papa Scratch staggered back, spat blood and grinned. "That's more like it, Rodney boy! Show me you got a little lead in your pencil."

"Give me what I want or I will *end* you."

Papa Scratch spat out more blood and whipped out a new toothpick from nowhere. "Okay, okay. Let's make a deal. I'll give you what you want, but you gotta do something for me."

Rodney took a step back.

Papa Scratch clicked his teeth together three times on his toothpick. "You gotta *meet* dear ol' daddy-o."

"What?" Rodney couldn't have heard that right.

"Just a little howdy-doo with your deadbeat progenitor."

"Why?"

"Why does everyone assume I've got some kind of vested interest? Because it'll make you happy. I just want to make all y'all *happy*."

Rodney took a step back. "No. Not him." He turned to go.

"Wait, wait." Papa Scratch's face was fallen when Rodney turned back around. "You're right. Maybe it won't make you happy. But I just gotta make sure you understand the terms of our deal, dig? You'll be following in daddy's footsteps, so I feel responsible to show you what might be in store for you, man. You good with that?"

Rodney took a step forward and nodded once. He could almost feel the music flowing from him.

"Cool, man. Cool," Papa Scratch said with his yellow eyes twinkling. He walked up to Rodney, who towered over him almost comically. The long fingers reached behind Rodney's ear and pulled out a tender, flickering blue light. Rodney barely noticed. His eyes had already blurred, maybe with tears, in anticipation of finally knowing the man who engendered him and the place from where he came. Or maybe time was already starting to fold and tear, to break not along the seams, but where Papa Scratch dictated it should break.

When his eyes cleared, Rodney was no longer standing at the crossroads. He was no longer anywhere. He looked around and saw only red-streaked rock under a red sky, glared at by a bloodshot red sun. A sound filled his ears, high-pitched and brutal. It drowned out all thought. It was all there was in this place. The screaming.

Rodney felt Papa Scratch's hand on his shoulder. He couldn't quite make out what the man was saying, but his long finger pointed to the ground. Rodney looked down. At his feet were the twisted and tormented faces of a hundred thousand men, women and children. They were screaming and bleating out of their locked jaws and out of their distended eyes. Skeletal hands reached out for Rodney and grabbed at his now torn and bloody ankles.

Papa Scratch leaned in close to Rodney's ear. "See that one right there," he said pointing a long finger at one of the tortured faces. "That's dear old daddy-o."

No. This was wrong.

In a breath, Rodney found himself beside his father and the screaming souls. He felt what they felt. He felt his soul being burned still within him. He pummeled his own gut with his giant fists, but that only broke his bones – it didn't end the pain.

"No!" Rodney shouted at Papa Scratch. "No! No, I don't want it – take it back!"

The screaming stopped and the place snapped into ear-ringing silence. They were back at the crossroads in a light falling rain. Papa Scratch was grinning his wide-mouthed grin. He chuckled slowly.

"That, Rodney boy, is *exactly* what I wanted to hear. Are you saying you'd like to renege on our little deal, my boy?"

Rodney felt his face distort in the same churning, tortured way he'd seen on the soul of his lost father. "Yes," he whimpered. "I can't – I can't live with that." He fell to his knees in the mud.

"Capital. First rate. Alas, there's no way back. You can't un-see what you've seen. You can't un-ring that particular bell." Papa Scratch steepled his long fingers. "But there are, of course, a couple of ways out. One of them you're not going to like very much."

Rodney looked up. Flanking Papa Scratch was a pale toothless man squatting in the mud beside a black-haired woman. Rodney felt afraid. He blinked, and for a hair's breadth of a second he saw the pale man as nothing but a yawning mouth, and the woman as a midnight black raven ready to peck at his very being. He blinked again and they were human. Or seemed so.

"Yeah, you've probably got an inkling at what my hounds here can do, yeah? You wanna let your soul go through that? If you do, well that's entirely your prerogative, my man," Papa Scratch shrugged. "Or – and I'm just thinking out loud here – you could maybe join us? I could use a man of your … well, let's not beat around the bush. I could use a man of your *size*." He jabbed a long finger at Rodney's chest.

For possibly the first time in his life, Rodney Baraquin didn't flow headlong into his first impulse. Seeing the damnation of his father may have put some caution into his ways. He thought about his options. Death, followed by the excruciating agony he'd seen his father suffer, the torment he'd seen on all those burning souls in hell. Or serving *Le Djiable*. That could mean an eternity of utter power. A hundred thousand lifetimes of control, of meaning and of strength. It wasn't a choice at all.

Would it matter now if this is what the long-fingered man had intended all along? There was only one way out, and it led Rodney to a self with purpose, something he'd never felt before in his short life.

He didn't speak. He only nodded his assent.

Papa Scratch smiled and pulled out a switchblade. Rodney was afraid, but when the blade entered his gut, when it tore apart his viscera, he felt at peace. The torment of his eighteen years – a torment he'd never noticed before without any happiness to compare it to – yielded to the knife like lips to a lover's kiss. Rodney watched as his mortal body fell onto the sodden ground. He watched as the center of his being became something new, something solid and untouchable. He looked the same, only sharper, harder. He could now ramble across the mortal world, free until his master called him. He was free from the chains of human mortality and human morality. He was new.

As Rodney walked down the road, back to the town he'd fled from as a murderer, he felt silver, he felt like he was a part of perfection. Where the authorities blew open part of the levee to release the buildup of water, a sacrifice of dozens of human lives to save hundreds, the bloated, blue body of one of the unlucky floated to him. The dead man clutched a shiny new harmonica in his left hand.

Rodney tried to pry it free, but death wouldn't let go its grip. So he snapped each of the dead man's fingers off. Rodney blew into the harp, tasting the acrid, slightly sweet tang of death and rot. But the notes he played were pure and mournful, silver and perfect. He played the blues, and, through his new instrument, the blues played him.

It was this mournful, wailing mouth harp note that Rodney's victims heard seconds before their souls were snapped from their bodies. Soon, this was what he was, the single blue note that was the harbinger of damnation. Now, everyone just called him Blue.

10. CROSS ROAD BLUES

The stone-solid memories that made up my life softened and smeared, like paint running together in blending streams. But behind these melting memories was no blank canvas, only hard reality etched and carved deeper than the whitewash shell of life being rinsed from my mind. I had new memories – no, not new. I had *my* memories. They were glorious, they were embarrassing, they were mundane – but they were all *mine*. And I walked through them as if through the paintings at a museum.

There was a vast, muscular nothingness around me. All I saw were my own memories.

I saw an exasperated middle-aged man shivering in his pyjamas outside his own house while the police questioned his family about his fitness as a father. That was me. I saw a happy man playing on the beach splashing in the waves with a little girl. That was me. I saw a man in a hospital room holding a newborn and looking out at dawn breaking on the horizon. That was me. I saw a nervous young man flub his vows at the altar of the church as his bride tried not to laugh. That was me. It was all me. I knew it was true, but I didn't remember it. I knew it happened, but I didn't *feel* it.

Amid the blending of light and nothingness, I saw a door. It couldn't have been a real door. It was always there, always in the same spot in my field of vision, through all the memories I walked through. The same white door. This had to be something. This had to be what I was looking for. A way out of this nocturnal false life.

I opened it. I walked through.

I saw a vast, open plain, wide and unending, covered in dead grass twitching in a wind I couldn't feel. The sky was the liminal blue of just before sunrise or just after sunset, that time of frozen possibilities. I swear I could see the curvature of the earth against the boundless expanse.

And the door I had just come through was gone.

I stood gazing out on the expanse. I breathed deeply and slowly, the air moving easily in and out of me. I closed my eyes and just breathed.

I breathed and I walked. I congratulated myself a little for not panicking, whether that was my doing or not – after all, this was a little outside of my experience. But I thought of the Laura I'd left behind, and of the grief that dragged at her face. I could stay here for an eternity if it meant alleviating that. I thought of her daughter – *our* daughter – and of bringing her back.

I don't know how long I walked. I don't know that time even existed in this place, or in any place so devoid of everything. How was I even supposed to measure time in this great plain? There was only the unbroken emptiness and the unfelt wind.

And a long, thin wisp of smoke on the horizon.

How had I not seen that before? In this limitless plain, under this unending sky, campfire smoke should have been visible for hundreds of miles.

I got to the fire and held up my hands. It was warm. I'd been wandering for so long – days? weeks? or only minutes? – that I'd forgotten what warmth felt like.

"Fire in this place is good," I heard a voice from behind me say flatly.

I spun around to see a man, naked to the waist, emerging from a tent made of animal skin that I know hadn't been there before.

His long hair was pulled into two braids that draped across the skin of his dark chest. Metal discs hung from his ears, and his pants were made of what looked like coarse buffalo hide.

"I'm no one you need to worry about," he said, answering my unasked question. "My name's Willie Brown. In these parts. We met before."

Had we? Of course. The day Colin Ackerman beat up his girlfriend. The night Laura told me she was pregnant. "Right. I do know you."

He nodded slowly.

"I was wandering down by the river – what? Fifteen years ago? When it was just a place that collected junk and junkies. I wanted to know what to do about the baby on the way. If I should stay." I remembered his words exactly. "You told me I had a destiny."

"You do have a destiny." Still nodding.

"Yeah – my destiny to follow my art and painting. To transcend myself no matter what the cost. You really helped me that night."

He stopped nodding. "You are not who you are." He looked me up and down, then cast his eyes to the distant horizon. "And who you are doesn't belong here."

"And where's here?" I asked, cocking an eyebrow. I sounded distant and small.

"This is the place between places. This is where the spirits sing their songs, guiding man and woman along their broken and erratic paths. And yet, you, Wood Sweeney, belong here."

"No. I'm trying to get back. I was – I was in the wrong place. The wrong world."

"Sounds like you met Papa Scratch."

"Yes, I've known him for –" I wanted to say years, but I wasn't sure that was true anymore. How long had I known

Papa Scratch? I couldn't trust any of my memories. I knew some of them had to be true, but I didn't know which. "It doesn't matter. You're right. I'm lost. I made some mistakes. They brought me here. Isn't that all life really is? The place all the mistakes we make bring us to?"

Willie Brown just nodded slowly. "Papa Scratch wouldn't have left you here. I pray you didn't break your deal with him."

"I suppose I did." I hadn't thought of it like that. "What does that mean?

"It means he owns you," Willie Brown said. "It means he can make you into one of his spiritless creatures. His hounds. And if he doesn't want to do that, you will just become their plaything until your soul is torn, eaten and digested. I'm told it's not very nice."

I thought of Greta the farmer.

"What you saw was what will happen to you. You've broken your deal, devil slayer. You belong to the hellhounds now."

I tried to look stoic. "I suppose this is the only way, is it? There's no chance of an exorcism or something?"

Willie Brown just shrugged. "You're not possessed. You gave yourself of your own free will. A soul is owed. Yours, or the soul of someone who will take your place of their own free will."

"No. This was my mistake. I'll face it."

I heard a long, lonesome, drawn-out harmonica note on the unfelt wind. Mr. Blue must have had a backup. "They're here for you now," Willie Brown said. "They will not leave without you or someone else willing. What are you going to do, devil slayer?"

"Why do you keep calling me that? I'm no devil slayer. I'm barely even a normal person."

"None of us get to choose."

This was getting me nowhere. "How do I get away from here? How do I get back to the world?"

Willie Brown stared at me stonily. "Out and in are matters of perspective. You're here because you chose to be here. Choose to be elsewhere, and you'll be elsewhere."

Goddammit. I wanted to punch the smug, mystical bastard right in the jaw. "What help is that?"

He shrugged and looked me over. "I'm not sure you deserve any help."

I thought of Laura and Makayla. I thought about what I could have done if I'd been there. "I'm damn sure I *don't* deserve help." I looked to the twitching grass. "But I'm asking anyway."

"Hm." He pointed just below my waist. "You know how to use that thing?"

I raised an eyebrow.

"In your pocket. The phylactery."

I pulled out Mr. Blue's harmonica, and its reeds vibrated in my hand. "Um. I've tried." I pulled on my beard. "I've done some really funky things with time."

Willie Brown sighed. "Time is easy. The phylactery lives on breath. Breath is life. Life is everything. Life is even time."

"This harmonica can get me out of here, then?"

"It can show you a door."

"Can you show me how?"

"No."

"Oh." I paused. I waited. I raised an eyebrow. And lowered it.

"It's *your* breath," he continued. "Only you can breathe your breath."

I was skeptical, but a magic mouth harp with the power to transport me back to the real world would not be the weirdest thing I'd seen over the last couple days. I'd play along and see where this went.

No.

Not anymore. Playing along and seeing where things went got me into this. I thought about what Laura said to me – that I'd changed.

I needed to get to a world where I could see a Laura not broken and cracked open by suffering. Somewhere where I could see my daughter alive. It was time to start determining some things for myself. Starting with how to play this thing.

I brought the harp to my lips and blew a low note. The plain undulated and rumbled. That was a good start, but I still didn't see any door. I drew in on a high note, bending my breath as I did. The nerves of my fingertips spread out across the vastness of the plain and I felt for a door. I pulled in breath harder, bending the note lower and lower, bursting now and full of breath and space.

I gasped as I pulled the harp from my mouth. I still didn't see a door.

I saw mirrors. Dozens of mirrors reflecting me back. No, not mirrors. Mannequins. Mannequins with my face, all dressed differently. This one in paint splattered khakis. This one in a floral shirt, sunglasses and shorts. This one – strangely – in pyjamas and a puffer jacket.

I staggered when the last one socked me solidly on the jaw. This was no mannequin.

"Hey, hey. Come on. Please," was all I could manage to spit out.

He hit me in the gut and I doubled over, spitting bile onto my leather.

"You're nothing," he said over me. "You're the weakness I've been calling strength. You're the rot I've been calling health." He shoved me, and I crumbled onto the red dust. "You're the hell I've been calling salvation."

He was right. I was sickness. I was corruption. I was soullessness.

He was right, but that didn't mean I was going to let him beat the living shit out of me.

I braced my feet against the red ground, threw my arm around his ankles and pushed.

He went down hard into the dust, winded. It was all I needed. I leapt onto his chest and pummeled out all the rage and hatred at my own indifference, my own passivity. I was done playing along and seeing where things went. I'd been chased, clawed at, my bones ground to meal. Now, I was taking this where *I* wanted to take it.

I hit him and I hit him and I hit him. He smiled through bloodied lips and missing teeth. With each blow, I felt my own face crack and soften, blood flying from open wounds – wounds that mirrored the ones I was inflicting – onto my pyjamas and puffer jacket. I was victim and assailant. I was slayer and slain. I was I vs. I. I turned my face to the sky and howled.

My wail shattered the night, sending shards of it raining down on me. The night-pieces tore clothes and rent flesh. A large blade of darkness pierced the left side of my ribcage, and I bled not blood, but deep blue, star-strewn night itself.

I howled again, and I could have sworn I saw a woman in a long, white dress watching me from a low hill.

With that vision, I felt a breath of frigid air bite at my cheeks. I looked around and was no longer on the vast, eternal plain of Willie Brown. I could smell pine and diesel, a wind bit at my face, and I felt a sharp pain in the left side of my chest.

I was at a railway crossing where the tracks intersected with a gravel secondary road. I recognized the place, but it was like I recognized it out of a dream or something. A *déjà vu* sense of having already been here but not remembering when. Or if it was even me who'd been here.

Like a slow-breaking winter dawn, the memories returned, cracking and shattering the false ones. I remembered the strangely carved bone, the deal with Papa Scratch. It all went down right here at these crossroads.

That bone! That was the key to all of this. If I could dig that up – if I could just have it back in my hand, maybe even destroy it somehow – then all of this could be over. I could negate all of this nightmarish voodoo shit.

Where did I bury it? I scanned the ground and saw an uneven lump in the gravel of the tracks. Gotcha.

I clawed through the gravel with my cold, aching fingers until they bled. I was down in the semi-frozen dirt, now in the clay. There was no bone. I was sure this was the place.

"You ain't gonna find it there, my man," Papa Scratch's voice said behind me.

I shot up and turned around to face him. "Let me out of the deal. I've made it this far. You know I can keep going. You know I can beat you. I'm the devil slayer." I was pretty sure that wasn't a bluff anymore. "Call off the hounds."

He shrugged and put his palms toward me, extending out his crab-leg fingers. "No can do, Woody, my man. A deal's a deal. Besides – you think I could call them off even if I *wanted* to? You seen those guys? Yeesh. They even give *me* the heebie-jeebies."

"I will *slay* you. You know I can. Find a way to get me out of this deal. You can find something."

Papa Scratch smiled broadly. "Well, of course there's *something*. You know that. All you gotta do is find someone to take your place. Take your place *willingly*, mind you. Easy peasy, right Mr. Big Bad Devil Slayer?"

That wasn't an option. I'd started this. I'd end it.

"How long do I have?" I asked.

As if in answer, I heard Mr. Blue blow a riff that echoed against the cold of the landscape. Wah wah-WAH wah wah. It sounded close.

"Well, since I like you so much, Woody, my man, I might be able to stall them a little bit. That is, if I can find a topic of conversation that would interest them. That Mr. Pale – not much of a talker."

It would have to do. I turned and walked quickly away from Papa Scratch without saying another word.

I covered the distance between the crossroads and my house faster than I would've thought. I barely noticed time passing. There was some higher force edging me along, filling my veins with steel and my bones with cold resolve. It was just past midnight when I got home.

Home. The word resounded like a bell in my weary brain. "I'm home," I whispered.

I opened the door quietly, and I crept upstairs. There was a light under Mak's door. I knocked gently and opened it.

She was in her heart-spangled pyjamas. I was sure she had the same pattern when she was a baby. She looked up at me and took off her headphones, and I could hear quiet, mournful music coming from them. "Dad?" she said, choking back tears. "I'm sorry. I'm sorry I ran off."

I sat down on her bed and hugged her. "Honestly, Mak? I would've done the same thing. I *have* done the same thing. Do you know how many times I've just run off in a tantrum when things didn't go exactly my way? When I didn't get to design the events around me? You got angry. It happens."

"Maybe you were right. We *should* take a vacation." She pulled away and looked up at me. "What's your vote?"

"Pitcairn."

Mak rolled her eyes. "We're not going to the Pitcairn Islands, dad."

"Think about it. It's the last overseas British Protectorate. What else could you want in a vacation destination?"

Her eyes rolled back farther than could have been comfortable. "Lots."

"But what about all that time I spent learning the language? What I am going to do with my Pitkern dictionary?"

She tried to roll her eyes back even farther, but human optical muscles don't bend that way. She broke a smile instead. "Dad!"

I could've held her like that all night. I wanted to. But I had other things to do.

I tapped my temple as I walked away. "Think about it."
I closed the door softly behind me.

Laura was waiting for me in the kitchen when I came downstairs. She looked at me. I looked away. We didn't speak. I stood at the door.

"Christmas, sixteen years ago," was all I said.

She hesitated for a moment. "What?"

I saw a softening spread across her face and took a step closer. "We'd just met, but you told me we'd get married and always be together. That you'd read the bones or thrown the cards or something. It was a bold move after four dates. But you asked me to trust you."

She came to me. I put my arms around her.

"It's me," I whispered.

She held me. "Is it?"

"Yes. Finally. It's me."

We embraced like that for a long time, and so much shorter than I would have liked. A clarion mouth harp note in the distance brought me back to myself.

"Look, Laura. I need to tell you something."

She looked worried. It almost made me stop. But she needed to know. After all we'd been through – even if she had no memory of that, even if this wasn't the same Laura – she needed to know.

So I told her.

I told her about Papa Scratch, about the other world, about the deal I'd made. I didn't tell her about the women. I didn't tell her about the other Makayla, or about the other Laura. I didn't tell her that I'd be free and clear if someone willingly took my place.

"And now I'm expected to become one of them. Of the hellhounds. Or not."

Laura's eyes lit up. "Wood, what are you saying? Have you been drinking again?" She stood up, lit a candle with a long match and breathed in its smoke.

The familiar acid rose in my gut. She needed to trust me about this.

No.

I needed to *get* her to trust me about this. With a story like this, burden of proof was squarely on me.

"Laura, look. I —"

She screamed ragged and high. My eyes followed hers out the window, and I saw Mr. Pale clinging upside down to a drainpipe outside the house and licking the kitchen window, leaving greasy, yellow stains that dripped down the glass.

In a motion, I picked Laura up where she screamed, set her at the archway to the living room and was out the back door, confronting Mr. Pale.

I was going to chase this ungodly beast from my house. I just didn't know how yet.

I made a cross of my index fingers and held it out to him with a stern look. He coughed out a cat-with-a-furball sound from the back of his throat and rolled on the ground, slapping his chalky knees with his hands.

So crosses didn't work.

He leapt to the roof of the garage and scampered out of my sight.

I remembered how he played with Greta the farmer.

I reached out for the nearest thing I could use as a weapon and found a cheap, plastic snow shovel. It would do. Well, I knew for sure it *wouldn't* do, but it made me feel better just holding it.

Something scratched on the snow behind me. I spun around, but I only saw a blur of white as Mr. Pale leapt over the fence. I heard him scamper down the alley and the familiar harp riff of Mr. Blue. Wah wah-WAH wah wah.

I stood with the snow shovel in both hands, knees bent, and I strained to hear anything in the preternatural quiet of the falling snow.

The back door opened, and I raised my weapon, ready to pummel that freak more thoroughly than I had my evil twin. I caught myself before I shattered the cheap plastic on Laura's wide-eyed face.

"Wood – what the hell?!"

"Hell is right."

"No. You weren't telling the truth. You were just playing some kind of cruel joke with all this devil deal talk."

"Laura. You saw the hound."

"No."

"Laura. It's me."

"So you're serious?"

"I told you."

"You made a deal with the devil and now that creature is after your soul."

"I'm sorry."

Her back straightened. "Don't be *sorry* – tell me what you're going to do about it?!" She was shouting now.

"Something! I'm going to do *something* about it!" I shouted back.

"What?!"

"I don't know!"

"Is there a way out?"

"Yes," I whispered.

"Then you'll do that."

"No."

"No?! You most certainly will, buster. You got yourself into this, get yourself out."

"No."

"Why?"

"Because someone would need to take my place."

She was silent.

"And don't even think about doing it yourself. I'm not going to lose you. I've just found you again."

"I'll do what I want. If it means saving you –"

"No – not going to happen, darlin'. You don't get to martyr yourself here. I made the deal, I'll pay the price. No one is going to stand in for me. I'm going to go to that spot, where the old tracks cross secondary highway 432, stand out in the open and face those goddamn hellhounds."

I heard a noise on the stairs, but by the time I got back inside, Makayla had grabbed a coat and was running out the front door. How long she been listening?

"Makayla!" But she was gone. I heard the car start and crunch out onto the snowy streets. I knew where she was going. I grabbed my puffer jacket.

11. HELLHOUND ON MY TRAIL

We were out the door and running along the icy roads into the increasing snow – slipping and falling occasionally, causing the wound in my side to bleed more night into the December dark – and I wondered how the hell we were going to get out to the crossroads on foot before Makayla got there in the car.

I fumbled with my phone and called a cab.

"We can certainly get a taxi to your location, sir," the slightly frazzled-sounding dispatcher said as Laura stared at me with pleading eyes. "But we're looking at twenty to thirty minutes. Is that alright?"

"What? No! I need to be – I need to be on the road *now*."

"I'm sorry, sir. But we're always busy just before Christmas. I suggest you –"

I hung up. I had one shot left. I stuck my hands into the pockets of my puffer jacket. I didn't know if it would be there. I'd left it in my leather.

And in another dimension. Do magical mouth harps transfer with consciousness between worlds?

No, it seemed. They don't. My pockets held only a crumpled receipt and a coin.

I started running again. That was all I had left. I knew we'd be too late.

I heard the rattle of Willie Brown's shopping cart and stopped. If I had any chance of making it to the crossroads before Makayla, I needed supernatural aid. And Willie Brown was about as supernatural as they come.

He stared at me with clouded eyes. "You don't look so lost anymore."

"I'm not. I know what I have to do." I sniffed in a lungful of cold air. "But I don't know how."

"Hm," he said and reached into his crinkled lingerie bag, shifting things around. He pulled out a grime-streaked vodka bottle, unscrewed the cap and took a long swig. He put the cap back on and put it away.

"You got anything else in there?"

Laura glared at me. "Wood, what are you doing? Mak's out there alone."

"I need the … phylloxera. Philoctetes." I cocked my eyebrow. "Help me out here."

"Phylactery?"

"That's the one!" I held my hand out to her. "Trust me. You told me four dates into our relationship that the universe wanted us to be together. I believed you. I played along with that for a long time to see where it went. But now, I'm not playing anymore. I'm going to defy the universe. As of tonight, I'm no longer with you and Mak because it's cosmically ordained. I'm with you because I *choose* to be with you. If tomorrow The Powers That Be decide on a new whim that we shouldn't be together, I'll *still* be here." I straightened my shoulders, raised an eyebrow and looked into Laura's eyes. "I reject the cosmic order. I renounce all deals. I break all rules."

"Wood, you can't just –"

"I can. I'm the devil slayer." I shot a glance to either side and cleared my throat. "Apparently. And my friend Willie Brown just might be gracious enough to help."

I turned back to Laura. "I can't stay, and I can't explain. Please – I need your blessing. I need us to work together."

She swallowed hard and turned away. When she turned back, I barely recognized her. "Go," she whispered. "If you can do this, do it. If there's a way to." She cleared her throat. "If there's a way to bring her back, I need you to do it."

Willie Brown had other ideas "I'm not sure you deserve any help."

"I'm damn sure I *don't* deserve help."

"Hm." He fished into his lingerie bag and passed something to me. "You left this at my place."

I looked one last time at Laura. "Wish me luck."

"You were right," she said with the hint of weak smile. "We should have just gone on vacation."

I smiled. "Pitcairn will be waiting for us on the other side of all this." I blew steaming air through the now-familiar note combination. Two, slide to three, draw and flutter my hands.

The snow hung suspended in the air. Willie Brown coughed.

"Not good enough," he said.

I drew in harder and bent the note as frigid air bit at my stinging lungs.

"Not good enough."

I glared at him, but sucked in harder. I felt ice in my chest. The note plunged low. I was so full of breath I thought I would drift away on the December wind.

"Not good en–"

I drew in harder so I wouldn't have to hear him say it again. My chest felt like it subsumed my chin. I felt the note dip and reverberate with the pulsing inside me. And, as I pulled with the last strength in my lungs, the note and the vibration of my being resounded in tune and shook my bones, my nerve endings and down into my very cells, and past even my cells, into the luminous, not-quite-there quicksilver substance that I call *me*.

The vibrating reeds shook away everything that I was and everything that I've ever been, leaving me at first hollow and then cracked open into nothingness. I'd forgotten that Wood Sweeney ever existed. My mind was too full of falling the snow, growing the grass, breathing the wind and turning the earth. It was an immense job, keeping the entirety of the planet moving and living and breathing, but I did it. I didn't feel the cold as I slipped with a swimmer's grace through the frozen ground and rocks at the speed of thought.

My veins were the frozen roots of the dormant green world, my bones were the stones that supported the great human weight on the Earth, and my spine was the world tree itself, jutting from beneath the underworld into the heavens and supporting the entirety of creation.

Around me was nothing. And everything. And myself. Because I was all things and all things were me. It was blackness and light, all things and the negation of all things. But ahead of me I saw a long column of light, a brutal beam bisecting a chunk of rock in the nothingness. I swam toward it through the thick nullity.

And then I was human scaled again. I had limbs, trunk, head. I was dressed in the skins of animals, and I smelled of wood smoke.

I knew this place. It was a great plain, covered in grass that waved in no perceptible wind and burned smokily in patches. This was the plain of Willie Brown. It was the place of endless spaces stared at by an empty sky.

And I was lost in it.

I knew it would take me years – if time had any meaning in this place – to find a way out. But Makayla didn't have years. She had minutes. She was going to the crossroads to hand over her soul in exchange for mine. An anger seeped through my skin at the thought.

In the twilit blue of the plain and the grey of the smoldering grass, something colorful caught my eye. A scrap of dark blue cloth, caught on a clump of grass and quivering in the unfelt wind. I looked closer. It was emblazoned with multicolored hearts – white, yellow, pink, red, then repeat. A child's pyjamas. Mak's pyjamas. Now and when she was a baby.

I dug with raw fingers into the grass and dry earth, pulling at rotting roots and gagging on the smell of corruption. I dug until my hands bled, and until I had no hands left. I dug with stumps of arms, deeper into the stony ground, until all that constituted me was this act of digging. All that I had become was force of will – the will to dig a way out of this unholy place. And then I became the very ground I was digging through.

I felt more than saw everything. I knew the logic of stones and the lament of snow that it must fall. I sang the myth of spring that comes to slay the frozen world, and the myth of cold misery that clouds a perfect summer day. I *was* all these things. I was God or Gaia or Papa fucking Smurf – whatever you wanted to call the mystical perfection that permeated the world and that could only be glimpsed from the corner of the eye – I was it. The beginning and the end – the alpha and the omega – begged my permission to end and begin. The sun bent to me on fiery knees, and the moon and the mountains were my mistresses.

And then none of it ever happened. It was washed and scrubbed from me like the fall of some last note of music into oncoming silence. I was nothing again. I was less than I'd been. Less than I'd ever been. The once so physical sensations of perfection rode away from me on the back of a black betty mare.

But I was whole again. I gasped. I was me. Out of the frozen ground, the gravel and out of the air itself, I was remade and returned to what I called the world.

And I was at the crossroads.

I saw the car – my car – pull up and heard it crunch the compacted snow. And I heard the long, wailing, bent note from Mr. Blue. My enemies had nearly overtaken me. My stomach revolted against the thought of them, and the slash in my ribs shot pain down nerve endings. I walked to the car to get Mak out of here.

I saw someone in the passenger seat, but I couldn't see who it was with the headlights pointed at me. I only saw the outline of the head. And of a hat.

No. She can't be with him. How had he –?

But questions were meaningless. It was Papa Scratch.

I altered my course, running now, and skidded up to the passenger side, flying the door open.

"Get out," I growled at Papa Scratch. "Get away from her."

He grinned and twirled the toothpick in his teeth. "Now, now, Woody, my man. Is that any way to talk to your old bestest pal?"

I reached into the car and grabbed him by the tie. I had no idea what I was going to do when I got him out of the car, but I wasn't ruling anything out. The devil had been talking to my daughter. I was pissed.

As my fingers clutched the fabric of his tie, a large white blur moved in my peripheral vision and thumped down on the roof of the car. I looked up and saw Mr. Pale crouched above me, snapping his head from side to side and grinning his toothless grin.

I let go of Papa Scratch and backed off.

Papa Scratch stood up slowly and petted the shorn head of Mr. Pale. "I don't think there's any need for violence, Woody, my man," Papa Scratch smiled. "But if *you* think there is a need for violence – well, Mr. Pale would be happy to oblige."

"Get away from her," I spat. "What did you say to her?"

Papa Scratch gestured with his thumb to Makayla, who sat motionless in the driver's seat with her hand still on the steering wheel. "This fine young lady? She's a good kid, Woody, my man. She certainly loves her daddy quite a bit. She would do anything for you. *Anything.*" He smiled broadly and ran his tongue over his top teeth. "She'd even give up her own soul to save yours."

"No. Undo it. I take back the burden. It's mine – not hers. I made the deal, let the hounds come for me."

Papa Scratch chuckled. Even Mr. Pale shook his bare, white chest and coughed out a sound that might've passed for laughter. "No can do, Woody, my man," Papa Scratch said as he caught his breath. "She willingly accepted. She told me so. She told me that she, Makayla Sweeney, did willingly take the place of one Wood Sweeney. That's all I needed to hear."

Ms. Fallen seemed to materialize out of the newly falling snow. She opened the driver's side door and helped Makayla out of the car. I watched the snowflakes as they fell and disappeared into the multicolored hearts on my daughter's pyjamas. She was still just a kid.

Papa Scratch had it all figured out – I wouldn't be surprised if this little trap was in his plans right from the beginning. To turn a fifteen-year-old girl into one of his twisted, unholy hellhounds. My girl.

That thought sparked a hard, defender-of-family rage in me that went deeper than the oldest part of myself. It was time. I reached into my pocket and whipped out the harp with more force than I meant to. I saw something silver roll down the road, but I was focused on Papa Scratch.

I drew in a long breath on a low note, bending it, and the frozen ground around the crossroads heaved and buckled.

Papa Scratch stumbled and caught himself. His toothpick fell into the snow.

That got his attention.

"Hey, man!" he called out with only a few scraps of his usual cool. "Some of us are trying to *work* here." He looked at me sideways and his tongue whipped out a new toothpick. "How'd you learn to do that, anyway? Anything else you can do, or was that a fluke?"

I drew in again and slid up a few notes, fluttering my hands as I went. The night poured into the earth, filling the ground we were standing on with emptiness and forcing all solidity up above us.

That one surprised me.

I pulled the harp from my lips, and nature reasserted itself. Violently. Papa Scratch and the hounds fell hard on the snow, and Mak knocked her shoulder against the car. Oops. Sorry, sweetie. Ms. Fallen rubbed a thin-fingered hand down my daughter's back.

Papa Scratch took a couple steps toward me with hands raised like he was surrendering in an old-fashioned cowboy movie.

"Wow, man. Just *wow*. That's some impressive chops." He put his hands down and clicked his teeth together three times. "You looking for a job? I could use someone with your talent. The hours are hell, but you can't beat the benefits." He shot a leer at Makayla. "I could even see my way to letting the little girl go. If you joined me."

Damn. I'd done it. I'd saved Mak.

So why didn't I feel victorious? I thought of Greta. I thought of the multitudes Papa Scratch lured into these hellish deals. For the first time, I realized even the foul hounds must have been people once, with the same hopes of a better life that I had. The same hopes of staving off the blackness that had led me to my deal with Papa Scratch. What if I could save more than just Makayla? What if I could slay him?

Oh, crap. I wasn't actually going to go through with this, was I?

"No deal." I spat. "You'll let us both out of the bargain and leave this place. Or I send you back to hell."

"Woody, Woody, Woody. Why you gotta be like tha–"

I had the harp to my mouth before he could finish. Blow two, slide to three, draw and wow.

The snow hung again in the air. Ms. Fallen's hand froze on Mak's back.

Papa Scratch clapped four times slowly. "Nicely done, my man." He stood in front of Mr. Blue's face, looking up at the giant man. "And come on – you too, man? I mean – it's *your* instrument for fuck's sake!" He looked back to me and shrugged. "But I ain't got time for this." He whistled through his teeth, and the snow fell hard on me again.

I moved the harp toward my lips, but it never made it.

Both my arms were held firmly and painfully by the giant paw hands of Mr. Blue. I could smell sulfur – brimstone – radiating from him, and I could hear his low mirthless laugh.

I should have taken the damned deal.

"Let her go!" I screamed once then repeated in a whisper. "Let her go."

I looked into Makayla's eyes. She looked scared, but there was an anger there, as well. There was a fierce, primordial rage that I'd only ever seen before in – well, that I'd ever only seen before in myself. It was determination. She was ready to do whatever needed to be done. I guess that meant I had to be, too

"Makayla," I said with as much calm conviction as I could while still being held hard by Mr. Blue. "You don't have to do this. You can just walk away. This is my problem, and I need to fix it." I started to choke on my words. "If you do this, you'll die." A tear tore off down my cheek and turned cold in the December darkness.

Her eyes stared back at me and mirrored mine with their own single tear. Her breathing got ragged. When she spoke, it came out with the same rage I'd seen in her eyes.

"No!" she shouted. "There are kids *dying* at my school. Of fentanyl. Josie DeLillo – I'd known her since kindergarten – is dead. And so many others. They all died meaninglessly. We all do. The news is calling it a pandemic."

"The news doesn't decide what you do. *You* decide."

"That's right! That's what I'm doing. I've *seen* it, Dad." she talked over me. "It gets everyone. If I'm going to die, then I decide I want my death to mean something. Why can't I make my death *mean* something? I can't save the kids at school. Why can't I just save *you*, dad? Give me at least that much." She gulped hard and added in a whimper, "Mak fix."

It dropped away – Papa Scratch, the hellhounds, the crossroads, the snow, the cold – all of it. There was only me and Makayla. She was all I could see, standing in front of me in her heart-spangled, little girl pyjamas.

I felt my heart pound, slow and stop.

I was in freefall between two worlds – between two aspects of myself. Sound muffled and faded away. I could taste the rural cold. I could hear the pulse of my blood.

The world came back in a sudden gust of wind. I turned to Papa Scratch. "Please. If your pet here wasn't holding me, I'd be down on my knees. I beg you. End this. Take me. Leave her alone. Please. *Please*."

Papa Scratch grinned and tongued a toothpick from somewhere in his mouth. "I wasn't kidding, Wood, my man. There's honestly not a darn thing I can do now. It's tough luck, but hate the game, not the player, you know what I'm saying?" He walked up to me, put a hand on my shoulder and brought his face close to mine. "Look, Woody, my man," he said with sulfurous breath. "I like you. I'll do you a deal. I'll make it easier on you. I'll make it so Laura, the grandparents, all of Makayla's friends – they won't remember her. It'll be like she never existed. Whoosh – gone off the planet. No grief, no suffering. Gee, Woody, ain't I good to you?"

I'd learned enough about Papa Scratch's deals to know that he never gave something for nothing. "Okay, so no one will remember her. What do I have to do for you?"

He laughed low and slow. "Well, it's not like *no* one will remember her. You, Wood – *you'll* have to remember. There won't be a day that goes by where you won't wake up with the image of your baby girl's eternal soul being ripped apart by my little beasties here." He whipped out another toothpick from somewhere. "That'll hurt, I bet."

"Why are you doing this?! What did I ever do to you?"

"I'm the fucking *devil*, man! What the heck did you expect me to do? I ain't gonna be all sweetness and light, now am I? This is what I am, my man. This is what I do. Said the scorpion to the toad."

Papa Scratch nodded at Ms. Fallen, who took out her carrion-smelling oil, dipped a finger in it and stepped toward Mak.

Something in me shifted. Only slightly, but fundamentally. In an instant, I could see everything that needed to be done, and I knew, somehow, that I could do it.

I almost smiled thinking about it, and Laura's woo-woo, cosmic stuff filled me with steel and determination. I was about to walk up to the devil himself, knee him in his goddamn balls, take my daughter and walk away. I felt myself grin as broadly as Papa Scratch ever had.

12. ME AND THE DEVIL BLUES

But it didn't go quite as I'd hoped. Does it ever when you're planning to genitally assault the Prince of Darkness and get your family back together?

I threw my weight back against Mr. Blue, who staggered and let go of me. Lurching forward, I lunged at Papa Scratch, tightened my shoulder against my body and muttered a little prayer. I had no idea how close I was. I just closed my eyes and hoped really hard.

I pummeled into Papa Scratch's body, and I knew something was wrong. I'd miscalculated my trajectory and I'd only clipped his arm – I should've kept my eyes open. But it was enough to knock him onto the cold gravel of the tracks as my forward momentum sent me careening off into the sharp undergrowth.

I shot a glance back over my shoulder. The hounds – Mr. Pale, Ms. Fallen and Mr. Blue – were closing in on Makayla. I watched Mr. Pale run his tongue along his toothless gums.

Forget Papa Scratch. There was no time. I needed to get my daughter out of here, and I needed to do it now.

Ms. Fallen took out her bottle of rot-smelling oil and dipped a finger in it, while Mr. Blue wailed on his harp, and Mr. Pale panted and dribbled pale green drool from his toothless mouth. I hopped onto my feet, cutting my cold-raw hands on the thorns of some leafless bush, and ran at the three of them. I don't know how I calculated it this quickly – if I calculated it at all – but I knew I had to go for Ms. Fallen. If I could stop her from getting that foul oil anywhere on Mak, I might still have a chance to save my daughter.

My body's full weight collided with Ms. Fallen, and she sprawled onto the ground, smashing her jaw against the cold steel of the railroad tracks with a muffled crunch. The bottle of oil shattered on the gravel, anointing nothing but stones and snow and dirt.

In a motion, I used my momentum to alter my course a little, grabbed Makayla around the waist and hefted her up on my shoulder. I dashed a quick look behind me – Mr. Blue and Mr. Pale were stunned and unmoving. Ms. Fallen stood up, her jaw hanging off the side of her face on cords of dry flesh. I turned back around and kept running.

But adrenaline's a tricky thing, and running down the road with a hundred-pound teenager on my shoulder was starting to make me feel my age. I could hear my breath rasping in my throat, and I lost sensation in my legs, feeling only the steady *boom boom* my heavy footfalls made on impact.

I looked back. Mr. Blue and Ms. Fallen – her dangling jaw swinging like the gallows with each step – were walking after me with mocking slowness.

I turned back around and saw a flash of ashen white – then collided with something hard at speed and felt the frigid slap of the cold ground on my face and chest.

Mr. Pale snapped his head to the side and hissed his rattling laugh. The frozen dirt sucked out whatever hope I had left of getting Mak out of this. I watched it ebb away like the last flames of a winter fire – trying to burn, but sputtering and smoking into darkness.

Makayla was already back up on her feet. The red streaks of tears fallen and then frozen marked her face, but she held her chin up high, just like when she got out of that police car a lifetime ago.

"Dad?" she ventured timidly. "Daddy?"

She didn't say it, but I knew. I knew what she was asking. Dada fix.

It wasn't a question – it hadn't been a question for Mak when she was two years old, and it wasn't now. It wasn't a sad child asking a parent – the personification of making everything better – to mend a broken toy. No. It was an *imperative*. She'd been *telling* me what to do. And now I needed to do the same. I needed to tell myself what to do.

Dada fix.

I hated all of it. I hated the voodoo and the devilment and the deals. Always with the goddamn deals. They were bigger than me They always had been. I'd been betting against the house at Vegas odds.

And I'd lost.

I lay there and slowly opened my eyes, unaware I'd even closed them.

I didn't know if I could get up. I was emptied out of everything I had. Every last part of my being had gone into attacking Papa Scratch and saving my child from the hellhounds. I didn't have enough left to get up. I'm not sure I had enough left to even breathe.

They say when you're about to die your life flashes before your eyes. I don't know about that, but I know that when I was about to watch my baby girl's eternal soul be digested and spat out by these unholy monsters excruciatingly painfully, I made a decision to look back over some of the deals I'd made that got me here.

The deals.

I opened my eyes. Papa Scratch had made a deal with me. Not the one that brought me here. Not the one that condemned Mak's soul. He'd made a deal with me in the other place – in the other life. I'd saved him from Kenny the quarterback kicking the living snot out of him. And he'd given me something for that act – the token of a promise –

something that I hoped would be as binding to him as all his damned devil-dealing was to me.

The coin. The token redeemable for his one unrefusable favor. It had to work. I didn't have another option.

I reached into my pocket with the last tension I had in my ache-riddled arms. There was nothing there. Both my pockets were empty save the mouth harp. The damn coin must have fallen out when I fell. Or worse – fallen out in the scuffle and been flung or kicked into the snow and underbrush. No. Please tell me it's not be back at the crossroads. Please.

Mr. Pale was scampering around Mak's feet and licking her legs. Mr. Blue and Ms. Fallen had caught up to us.

I took the harp from my pocket and breathed a breath through it that steamed in the Christmas cold, sending clouds to block my vision. I breathed out the dust and the dry death of the last few days, cast them out of my body with a single, long rasp. It felt like a last breath – a death rattle. And maybe that's exactly what it was. Maybe this was the death of who I was. The death of who I'd been. R.I.P. the sad, middle-aged man, afraid of his wife. The man who needed to deal with the devil and risk his very soul just to see if he would have been happier – no, worse, more *fulfilled* – if he'd done a runner, if he'd left his pregnant girlfriend and abandoned his only living child. That man died that night. And I laughed. He was a coward and a loser. And he wasn't me. He hadn't been me for years. He was a costume, a shell, a hardening of habits through overuse, like the callous on an overworked finger. Hold your face like that for too long and it'll freeze that way. That's what my mother used to say when I was a kid. Turns out it was true. Hold yourself in a certain way too long and it becomes who you are. It becomes your life story. It makes you think that's you who are, but it takes so much energy to maintain, that all you think about is *you*.

That was the moment I died. It was the happiest moment of my life.

I'd done it. The hounds surrounded Mak, but they weren't moving.

My eyes darted around the ground I was still lying on, and my sense of sight seemed to have been multiplied. I could see everything from all angles at once. I could see Makayla staring defiantly at the hellhounds who were time-slowed but still moving slowly toward her, toward us. I could see Papa Scratch back where I'd knocked him down, now standing and dusting off his old-fashioned suit with those grotesque spider-leg fingers. I swore I could even see the crossroads of road and rail heave and lurch, as if nature itself was recoiling at the scene about to be played out here.

And I could see the coin.

Not three feet from me, in a small heap of dirty snow under a leafless shrub, was the coin Papa Scratch had given me – forced on me – with the words *you get one unrefusable favor from me*.

I finished my long, dry exhale and closed my eyes. My lungs were empty. My head was empty. My life was empty.

Dada fix.

I breathed in sharply. It was cool and wet, and it met the hot darkness inside of me with a sizzle. I might have screamed, but I don't think so – it was more a hiss that came from somewhere in the cells of my body, from the fluids and the spaces between everything that made up this solid form I called mine. I'd like to say I felt primal – like I felt I'd tapped into something ancient and perfect and powerful. But I didn't feel anything. I was pure motive, darting toward an aim, unconnected to the dragging forces of fear or hate or pity or love. I was action.

As pure action, I got to my feet, dove for the coin in the snow and pocketed it. Almost at the speed of thought, I was standing with the coin firmly closed in my right palm. I shoved my hands into my pockets.

"Papa Scratch!" I called out.

"Papa Scratch!" I called again. The hellhounds, still moving time-bent slowly, began to speed up. They turned and grinned broadly at me. I'm sure it wasn't the first time they'd seen someone beg for their lives. Or for someone else's. Only Ms. Fallen didn't smile, unable to with her jaw hanging half off her. The thought that I had done that to the nauseating she-witch filled me with a warm pride.

I called out again. "Papa Scra-!" but he was behind me, his too-long fingers on my shoulder, before I could finish.

"Come on, man," he said to me placidly, almost cooing. "Let it go. There's nothing more you can do. That's just the way the bee bumbles."

I stared at him, not in hatred, not in anger, and certainly not in fear. I stared at him from a point of perfect calm.

Papa Scratch's grin drooped a bit. Only at the corners at first, but soon, as I stared at him with the beatific Buddha-smile I felt spread across my face, he wrapped his lips into a pucker.

"You ain't gonna beg, are you, man?" he said, trying to regain his old grin but not quite getting there. "I usually like it when they beg. But you – aw heck, Woody, my man. We've been through so much together. I like you. I don't wanna see you beg."

I stared at him with my calm smile of repose. He wrinkled his brow and sneered a bit.

Papa Scratch's eyes scanned the winter sky, as if searching for some kind of half-gone memory.

"Hey man," he said, his teeth now fully bared in a mirthless smile. "I know she's your daughter and all, but, since her soul's about to be swallowed and slowly digested and all … well, you wouldn't mind if I had a little … taste first?" He slowly and carefully sucked each of his foul fingertips. "I do so like them at this age," he added, looking over at the speeding up Makayla.

I lost my place of stillness. He'd done it – he'd rattled me into anger and hatred. My plan wouldn't work if it came from emotion. I needed that perfect calm, that synchronicity of thought and act. I needed to get it back. But it was too late. I was already talking.

172

"You owe me one," I growled with far more anger than I'd wanted to.

"What? I owe you nothing. You got all the pussy you asked for, man. And a damn fine talent, to boot. Ain't my fault if you gave that all up. I don't owe you shit. But *I'm* still owed a soul." He turned to the trio of hellhounds and sighed. "Maybe we can speed this up a bit, my friends?"

"You owe me one," I said again, not quite strongly enough to cover the wobble in my voice. "You owe me one unrefusable favor."

"What?" Papa Scratch barely looked at me, keeping his yellow eyes on Mak. "Don't make this any harder on yourself than it needs to be, man. Come on. Have some dignity, pal o' mine."

I grabbed him hard by the shoulder. "You owe me a favor," I said, almost gleefully this time. "Cancel the deal. No deal. No soul."

Papa Scratch's eyes searched the ground, flipping the pages of his memory. I saw the exact moment he remembered. He knew it – the promise he'd made to me after I'd gotten his precious hide free and clear of that brick shithouse kid.

"I saved your life." I was smiling now. "That's binding."

"Woody, my man. you most surely did, but any favor I grant you has gotta be in my power to grant." He pressed his long fingers as if praying, still without making eye contact. "There's nothing that would give me more joy in this world than to release you, but that ain't something I can do. The dominoes are falling, pal. It's cosmic, dig? Bigger'n you, bigger'n me. Maybe even bigger'n the Big Guy." He waggled his fingers. "*Cosmic.*"

"Alright, then I'm not asking to break the deal. I'm asking for something else." I cocked an eyebrow and pulled on my beard. "Take my place."

His eyebrows shot up and the corners of his mouth plunged. Now he looked at me.

"Hey, come on, Woody, my man," he coughed. "That wasn't really the kind of thing I had in mind. I mean, sure I owe you a favor and everything. But – come on. This? You don't honestly think that I'd step in there, do you? You know how many times I've watched these cats suck out souls and chow down on them? It looks horrible. Just *really* unpleasant. You wouldn't do that to your old pal, now would you? After all we've been through?" He shivered, paused, then grinned again. "And it's kind of a moot point now, isn't it, Woody, my man? You'd need the coin." He clicked his spider-leg fingers together. "Can't do nothing without the coin."

The hellhounds circled Makayla, now all moving at normal speed. Ms. Fallen had a new bottle of oil – I could smell it from here – and I saw drops of it drip from her extended finger.

Mak looked to me with raw, primal, human terror in her wide, wet eyes. With my beatific repose covering my increasing doubt about whether this plan would work, I mouthed the words *dada fix*.

Ms. Fallen reached out an oil-daubed finger to my daughter's forehead, and Mak knocked it away, causing Ms. Fallen's nearly-severed jaw to pendulum violently.

"Nice *face*!" Mak spat at Ms. Fallen and rolled her eyes in full fifteen-year-old-girl glory. That's my girl!

It was time. I crossed my fingers and hoped all this woo-woo cosmic stuff and its arcane rules were on my side – *our* side – for once.

I wrapped my hand tight around the coin in my pocket and pulled it out. I held it with fully extended arm into his smug face.

Papa Scratch just grinned.

Crap.

I'd made a mistake. I must have. Why did that surprise me? Who was I? Wood Sweeney, normal guy. I was no slayer of devils. I worked at a real estate firm, for Christ's sake.

"Wood, Wood, Wood," Papa Scratch sighed. "You just don't get it, do you? The dealer always wins." He leaned into me. "And I'm the dealer, in case you didn't follow my little analogy. I'm the fucking king daddy dealer of them all! Chuck that trinket away. It's meaningless. You think I'd give you that kind of control over me? Come on, man. You're better than this."

Fuck. What now? The coin had to be key. I just needed to find the right keyhole, and I needed to find some inspiration for that from somewhere. Fast.

I stuffed my hands into my pockets, the coin with them. Papa Scratch's eyes followed it before coming back up to lock with mine.

I'll admit it. I was desperate. I was at a loss. He'd conned how many thousands of poor wretches out of their immortal souls? And I was an absolute beginner in this world.

But I had one advantage over him. I had nothing to lose. Not anymore. I'd lost my wife once. I'd lost my daughter once, and I was about to lose her again in a way far more horrific and meaningless than a fentanyl overdose. And I was going to have to watch it happen. No, I had nothing to lose. That made me dangerous.

The ancient pounding started again, as familiar as my heartbeat, and it drove me to a goal. I knew that, when I achieved it, the thing I called *me* would no longer be necessary. When that time came, nothing would be able to keep me together. Until then, nothing could stop me.

I had a feeling that was no feeling at all. Feelings only came from the friction of soul against purpose, the resistance of dream against reality. There was no friction now. There was no resistance. My soul and his purpose were aligned, and I was nothing but intent as I walked toward Papa Scratch at the crossroads at the edge of town. My feet only existed as they hit the ground. My body only existed as far as it held the coin. The ground itself, the snow and the frozen dirt, only existed to support me.

I couldn't stop my eyes from darting around. Papa Scratch was still grinning. The trio of hellhounds still circled the now-anointed Mak. The earth itself still seemed to heave at the unholiness of what was going on.

But, no. Something was different. Something subtle.

I looked back at Mak and the hounds. None of them – not Mr. Blue, Mr. Pale or the wretched, jaw-swinging Ms. Fallen were looking at my daughter anymore. They were looking at me. But not at my eyes. At my waist? No, no. Of course. They were looking at my hands in pockets. They were looking in the direction of Papa Scratch's coin.

Yep, I bet I could use that.

Papa Scratch was lying. Why else would these monsters care so much about the coin?

A giddiness blew across me, starting in my kidneys and radiating out to my fingers and toes – the warm, gently prickling energy that comes from sureness of victory.

The feeling that comes right before being kicked hard back down to the ground.

"You owe me a favor," I said one last time, mustering the limp remains of my cocksure arrogance. I must be forgetting some part of this. I had to be. There was something else that I needed to make the whole thing binding.

Papa Scratch hung his head and laughed a laugh of ferocity and relief. He supported himself, hands on knees as sob-like guffaws rocked his body.

"Oh, Woody, my man," he choked out when he'd caught a small corner of his breath. "I can't do it anymore. I can't leave you on the hook. Of course the coin is binding. Of course I owe you an unrefusable favor. You're cute, man. I mean it. Just adorable." He dropped his smile suddenly. "So, seriously, what's it going to be? What favor are you going to ask of old Papa Scratch? You want the talent back? The girls? Yeah, you do. You want the girls again."

"Take Makayla's place. Let your pet weirdoes eat your soul instead. If you have one."

Papa Scratch's grin came back as suddenly as it had left. "Make me," he smiled.

Damn. I knew there was a missing piece to this plan. I knew there had to be some special incantation, some kind of magic words that would force Papa Scratch to take Mak's place. It would have to be the same magic words she would have said to take my place.

And I was pretty damn sure it wouldn't be *please*.

The seconds stretched like a rubber band – I spent a lifetime searching my adrenaline-flooded brain for a missing memory, for whatever incantation would fix all of this. Then the rubber band snapped, and time reasserted its steady, tyrannical beat.

And I still didn't know the magic words.

I turned to look back at Mak. I wanted that look to say everything. I needed to say to her that I was proud of her for what she was doing, and that I was pissed at her for what she was doing. That she'd live on with me. That I loved her. That I was sorry.

But she wasn't looking at me. Her eyes were locked on Mr. Blue, Mr. Pale and Ms. Fallen. It looked like she was trying to come up with some more snark to spit at the hounds but couldn't do it.

They didn't seem to notice. They were staring at my jacket pocket.

All the clarity of purpose and the tenseness of action left me, and my body slackened. My fingers opened and the coin fell to the ground. I fell hard on my knees, but the sharp stabs of the gravel felt distant, a memory of pain from long ago, separated from me by an eternal ocean of pure, red anguish.

I'd lost. It was over now. Mak would be turned into one of Papa Scratch's hellhounds, and I'd watch it happen. Another meaningless death.

I couldn't tell if I was still kneeling in the gravel or if I'd fallen over. I just remembered Mak. All of it. Every stupid power struggle, every half-failure of a family vacation, every time I'd wanted her to leave me alone when she wanted to talk, every time I tried to get her to talk when she wanted to be left alone. I remembered every time I'd failed her, no matter how small, right up to tonight. I remembered vividly Papa Scratch telling me that she, Makayla Sweeney, did willingly take the place of one Wood Sweeney.

Did willingly take the place of.

She, Makayla Sweeney, did willingly take the place of me, Wood Sweeney.

Magic words. An incantation.

I was on my feet before I felt myself stand. The coin was in my hand, and I held it toward Papa Scratch.

"Back off," I barked, turning back at the hellhounds. "Leave her alone." They all stepped a pace away from Mak.

Papa Scratch rolled his eyes. "Aw, come *on*, man! This again?" He knitted his long fingers together. "You're making a fool of yourself. You really are."

I wanted to let him know that I'd won, but I didn't miss a beat. I couldn't afford to. I needed to remember these words perfectly. I didn't have the luxury of gloating before I sent the devil back to hell. Shame – I probably wasn't going to get an opportunity like this again.

"Do you, Papa Scratch," I started and watched his insufferable grin droop. "Do you, Papa Scratch, willingly take the place of one Makayla Sweeney?"

Papa Scratch's shoulders fell. "No, I can't, man. No. No, I really can't," he stammered.

I took a step closer. "Do you, Papa Scratch, willingly take the place of one Makayla Sweeney?"

A faint blue glow started to emanate from the goat on the coin, growing in intensity until it lit the crossroads in what looked like bright, sweet daylight after a long night of the soul.

Again. "Do you, Papa Scratch, willingly take the place of one Makayla Sweeney?"

"Come on, Wood. *Please*. You can't do this. Have some pity. Why are you doing this?"

"Why am I doing this? How can you ask me that? You're the fucking *devil*, man! What did you think I would do, given the chance?"

The light flared, and Papa Scratch shielded his eyes with his arm, knocking his hat to the snow.

I kept going. "Do you, Papa Scratch, willingly take the place of one Makayla Sweeney?"

The hellhounds left Mak and moved with their agonizing slowness toward Papa Scratch. "Wood. My friend. These pets of mine – I maybe haven't always treated them as well I could have. Do you know what they'll do to me if you keep going with this?"

Nope. I didn't know what they'd do to him. But I sure as hell wanted to find out. "Do you, Papa Scratch, willingly take the place of one Makayla Sweeney?"

The coin in my hand was cool as a spring morning, but the blue light emanating from it intensified, now focusing its beam into a spotlight on the trembling form of Papa Scratch. Greasy smoke rose from his back and shoulders, and his body convulsed in angular spasms.

Louder this time. "Do you, Papa Scratch, willingly take the place of one Makayla Sweeney?"

Papa Scratch ripped at his face and pulled off long strips of skin with his spider-leg fingers, revealing greenish, maggot-writhing flesh beneath it. I heard Mak gasp.

I was shouting. "Do you, Papa Scratch, willingly take the place of one Makayla Sweeney?"

His face was naked now, a skull plastered with rotting flesh, but his eyes still stared out at me. They were pleading.

"Do you, Papa Scratch –"

"Yes! Yes, just make it stop!" he called out in a voice that wasn't his.

The coin burned to nothingness in a burst of sulphur. I spun on my heel and nodded sharply at Mr. Blue, Ms. Fallen and Mr. Pale. They moved with surprising swiftness to surround their once-master. I only had time to kiss Papa Scratch once on the forehead and whisper *thank you*.

I didn't want to look, but I did. It wasn't like the German woman that I'd seen them devour on the plains of hell. That was business. With Papa Scratch, they seemed to be enjoying it.

Ms. Fallen went in first, anointing Papa Scratch's rotten-flesh forehead with the foul oil. I could have sworn I saw tears streak down his skinless face.

The anointing done, Mr. Blue drew out one long, mournful note from his harp and moved in. He reached out his giant paw hands, grabbed Papa Scratch's arms, smiled once, and ripped them from the body in one explosive motion.

"Shit fuck Jesus cunt fuck bitch!" Papa Scratch shouted while his arms were wrenched off. As Mr. Blue did the same to his legs, Papa Scratch continued spitting out his trail of nonsense obscenities. I watched the legs tossed aside and tried to ignore the maggots that squirmed from their bare sockets.

Mr. Pale leapt in and squatted on Papa Scratch's chest. He plunged his frostbitten fingers into Papa Scratch and pulled out long, leathery strings of unrecognizable organs. Mr. Pale licked the dried offal and rubbed it across his chalky skin.

I thought of my father's cremation when Mak was five. I let her come then to get a basic understanding of death, but I didn't want her to see this. I turned Makayla around as Mr. Pale leapt naked in the empty cavity of Papa Scratch's chest. She didn't resist.

And then Papa Scratch burned. His hollowed-out torso went first, bursting into bright orange flame that lit up the old dirt road brighter than the coin had. He spat out his curses until his tongue burned. But in his eyes – did I see some kind of repentance there?

Maybe not.

Mak had turned toward the scene again. I put my arm around her as we watched the devil burn.

I don't know how long we stood there like that – certainly longer than it took for what had been Papa Scratch's body to be completely consumed by the flames. All that was left was his hat. Mak and I stood and stared at the black spot in the wild grass and scrub by the roadside.

Dada fix.

Mr. Blue came over to us first. I tensed, ready for a fight, knowing fully well I didn't have a chance against the giant hellbeast. But his manner was calm as he approached us, and his face was placid.

He placed one of his oversized hands heavily on my shoulder, and I flinched and winced at the sheer weight of it. He held out his other hand to me. It took me a minute, but I knew what he wanted. I reached into the pocket, passed him the harp and watched his thick fingers close around it. He looked me in the eyes and smiled. Not the grin he had when hunting his prey for Papa Scratch, but a peaceful, thankful smile that was punctuated by a knitting of his thick eyebrows.

He bowed, and then he was gone. He didn't walk away, he didn't get sucked up into the earth, he didn't even disappear. He was just gone as if he'd never been there.

I felt a tug at my sleeve and turned to Mak. She pointed at a stone, just off the side of the road in the low, bare scrub. A tombstone. I squinted to see the name. *Rodney Baraquin*. Of course Mr. Blue had a life before Papa Scratch. They all must have.

As Ms. Fallen came toward us next, I recoiled and pulled Mak close to me. Though I was pretty sure I had nothing to worry about, just the sight of her jaw still dangling from her head made me sick.

She pushed her jawbone back to its rightful place, tied it there with her scarf of ivory silk and stood on her toes. She kissed me. It took my breath away. Quite literally. It was a dry, dusty kiss that sucked the air from my lungs and probably took a few years off my life.

She untied the silk, causing her jaw to nearly swing off her face, and placed it around my neck. It felt pleasantly cool, even in the early December morning. Then she, like Mr. Blue before her, was gone as if she'd never been there. A bird cawed in the distance.

I felt Makayla tense at my side. Damn. It must be Mr. Pale's turn. But there was no solemn exchange. He only curled himself around my feet and licked the sides of my boots. His chalk-white skin had taken on some color, but that bare head and toothless mouth still creeped the hell out of me.

I looked down at the feral form of Mr. Pale, waiting for him to vanish from time or whatever happened with the other two. But he didn't. I kept waiting. He just crouched there, nuzzling my ankles.

"Go to the car, Mak."

She did.

I walked to the greasy stain that was all that was left of the being who called himself Papa Scratch. Mr. Pale crouched and creeped around my ankles as I did, but scampered away when I squatted down.

I picked up his hat and put it on. It was too small to wear on the jaunty angle that Papa Scratch wore it, so I cocked it on the back of my head. The wound in my ribs ached, but I felt I could fold up the darkness and cast it to burn against the oncoming dawn.

The car horn sounded. I stood up and slowly turned, shuffling along the gravel as I went. Mr. Pale nuzzled my ankles.

"Dad?" Makayla said when I got to the car. "Do you think I could ask a favor?"

I looked at her, glad to have a reason to look away from the last and oddest hellhound. "Of course, Mak. Anything."

She poked an accusatory finger into my sternum. "No more dealing with the frigging devil."

I laughed.

"I'm not kidding!" The finger jabbed a few more times. "No more of this. You had your little experimental phase – and that's perfectly natural at your age – but enough's enough. We're done here. I'm drawing a line under it." She poked at me again three or four times then took my hand. "Now I'm taking you home. I think I need to sleep for a few weeks before I'm able to deal with any of this." She wrapped her arms around me. "Ready for that vacation?"

"Pitcairn Islands, here we come!"

"Dad!"

"Seriously, though. Come spring, let's look into you taking your driver's test. If you can deal with this, you can deal with rush hour traffic."

Mr. Pale rubbed against the door. Mak looked at him, and he cocked his head like a lost puppy. I think she was considering letting him come with us.

I raised an eyebrow and gave her a half-stern look. She smiled, got in the car and closed the door.

Laura was waiting on the curb, bundled against the cold, when we drove up. She held Mak without words. I sat alone behind the wheel. I lifted the hat and put it back down on my head.

Laura looked at me over Mak's shoulder. Our eyes locked. I could have sworn it was still our fourth date – when she told me the universe wanted us to be together. I closed my eyes slowly and nodded. Laura led Makayla into the house.

I knew I should go with them. I wanted to. I didn't.

The pain in my left side flared and I put my hand to it, feeling the cool of night and starlight on the wound. I wondered briefly if it would ever heal. I didn't realize then that I didn't want it to.

I couldn't say how long I waited in the rapidly cooling car watching the light in the house. Slowly, I got out, shuffled along the walk and mounted the two stairs to the front door. I hesitated. I turned around, picked up a handful of snow and rubbed my hands with it.

Allowing a genuine smile to break over my face, I walked in the door and hung Ms. Fallen's silk scarf and Papa Scratch's hat on a hook.

The pain in my side flared again.

13. DEAD SHRIMP BLUES

Memories – if you could even call recollections of events that never happened *memories* – faded into the passing months, boxed up like the once-strong emotions of a dream, leaving only detail and nothing of their life-or-death urgency. I went back a few times to the spot where Papa Scratch burned. It was easy to find – nothing ever grew again in that place. For a while, I brought flowers to the grave of the being I only knew as Mr. Blue. But, like any ritual unconnected to living emotion, my visits became less frequent, and soon stopped entirely.

When Mak turned sixteen in the early summer, all that was left was a dark blue knowledge of how fragile everything was. What if this life – family, warmth – was part of a deal made by another, infinitely sadder version of myself, living alone in a cat-piss bachelor apartment across the river in some alternate dimension far too close to our own? Could I trust anything? What did I have to do, and what did I have to avoid doing to keep this bubble of the good life intact?

That was the blue note under the rattle of my everyday as I passed my days in planning and work and eating and errands and all the motions you go through to make a life.

My wound bled night when the wind came on strong, but mostly I just got on with my life.

I was a graphic designer among real estate agents, subject to interminable dinner party conversation about house prices and forced to meet awkward, spotty boyfriends and drive them home after Mak's movie dates.

I loved it.

I grew my beard longer and bushier. I thought it looked appropriately rugged after slaying the devil and everything. I wasn't sure Laura was impressed.

It was a cool evening in September when the wound in my ribs bled more nighttime than usual. I held my hand against it, trying to keep the other world separate from my quotidian existence, and I eased myself into the give of the couch, hanging my feet over the edge. I wanted to be content. Everything around me should have hummed contentment in my happy ears.

My leg bounced beside me. I watched it jitter. I knew what could nullify this kind of restlessness. I glanced at the bottle of Ballantine's on the shelf. I glanced at the door in the direction of Laura and Mak. No. Not that.

One more time to the place where he burned.

"Laura?" I called out. I poked my head into the hallway. "Laura?" Quieter now.

I grabbed a leather jacket from the closet – had I always had this jacket? – threw a bag of Laura's granola into the pocket and opened the front door. "I'm going out for a bit." I was nearly whispering now.

I fished in my pocket for the car keys. No. Better to walk. I'd find that old railway line and follow it out there. I'd like to say I thought deep and hard about my position in the world and about what I'd done for the good of humanity. But all I thought about was the life I left behind. There was a blue uneasiness creeping up on me. An uneasiness that came from my gut, up my spine, and into the back of my brain, gnawing on shrunken half-memories and causing them to swell to full size again.

I thought about the life – the half-life – that I'd left behind. The painting. The women. I'd never want any of it back, but I missed it. I tried refusing to admit that, but I missed it.

I crossed from road to tracks and kept walking.

The crossroads came on me like finding what you're looking for in a dream – perfect and perfectly unexplainable.

The late summer foliage grew in a Papa-Scratch-shaped outline around the bare, greasy earth where he'd burned.

"Hi," I said, surprising myself. "I know you're not here, and I know that's because of me – it's just that. It's just that I don't have anyone else to talk to. No one gets it. Not their fault, of course. No one else *can* really get it, can they? I mean, there's no support group for devil slayers, is there?" I pulled on my beard and raised an eyebrow. "Wait – is there? No, nevermind."

I took a step toward the greasy dirt.

"I miss it." Hollow panic shot through my gut. "Not that I'd want it back or anything. But I miss the eeriness of it all – the tingle at the base of the skull from all that weird, devil stuff. The deals and the binding and the hounds and all of it. Am I being nostalgic for a lost hell? I don't think so. It's just the excitement. It's the feeling that I was cut out for something better in life. Like I was cut out for greatness. Laura would call it *destiny*." I coughed into my arm. "Jesus. I hope I've learned to avoid that word."

A motion in the corner of my eye flickered in time with a scrape of metal on stone, and I shot my attention to it. Something glinted at the foot of Mr. Blue's – no, Rodney Baraquin's – gravestone.

I knew what it was before going over, but still I went.

The harp. Crap. The one I'd given back to Mr. Blue. I suppose this is what I asked for. I said I missed this world of devil-dealing and hellhounds, and this is what I get. A way back in.

I turned back to the place where Papa Scratch burned. "But this time I'm casting my lot firmly on the side of the angels." I coughed. "Did you hear me?" There was nothing. Not even the wind.

"Screw it." I bent down and picked up the harp.

In a wave that came on like nausea, my nostalgia deepened and dug in, and I imagined I heard the low, mournful wailing of that instrument – the sound that was harbinger of all the black magic I'd fought so hard against, but which was the source of my own magic, and, at this moment, the very thing that gave my mundane life any meaning in the tidal swells of suburban ritual and nine-to-five surety. I hadn't realized how much I'd needed the devil dealing. And how much I needed to resent it.

I picked up the harp and turned it over in my hands. Its metal was strangely warm in the evening cool, and it vibrated low.

I brought it to my lips. No, that's not entirely accurate. I *allowed* it to bring itself to my lips with its gentle tug – like a Ouija board pointer, a force I knew I could resist, but a force that emanated from somewhere not me.

I blew. The taste of dust and old gumbo filled my mouth.

It was just a little puff of air, but the harp let out a long, slow note that bent in the middle. There was no way my breath made that note.

The night poured from the slash in my side and filled the crossroads with distant stars, hollow winds and black. As I breathed in again over the reeds, I bent the note, and with it bent the nighttime and swirled it into helixes of my own choosing.

I stopped. The night poured back into my wound. I cast my eyes from side to side. I strained to listen. I heard nothing.

I tried drawing in air through the harp again, bending the notes, and the night inside me flowed against the trees and the gravel, stretching them to celestial expanses.

And in the swirl of night, I saw a place atop a high hill, surrounded by dry scrub and rocky soil.

A whisper that wasn't heard as much as instinctively understood said *La tumba del diablo*. The Devil's Grave.

I pulled the harp from my lips and the swirl of blackness retreated into my side.

With the harp clutched so tightly its edges cut into my hand, I called out to the place where Papa Scratch burned. "No! This is not my world. This isn't who I am. Is there some kind of magic incantation I need to say to get rid of all this voodoo stuff? *I, Wood Sweeney, do solemnly renounce all this damn tedious, spooky, Hallowe'en-y crap.* Did that do it?" There was nothing.

With full deliberation, I aimed carefully and flung the magical, time-slowing mouth harp into the densest copse of trees. Its reeds vibrated as it flew, and the slash in my side bled deeper darkness into the night. I heard a simultaneous thud and crack.

"Now that's done, and I'm glad it's over," I said without looking at the bare Papa Scratch earth.

The helpless wail of a child cracked through the falling silence, and my full being tensed, ready for whatever hellish goblin I'd conjured with that throw. I really need to know when to quit.

A randomly bouncing flash of white bounded onto the tracks and bleated again.

Right. The goat.

I crouched and held out a handful of granola. The goat nearly licked the skin off my palm in its hunger. "Well," I said, scratching between its ears. "I can't leave you out here, can I?" I pulled on my beard. "Though you've been fine for the last nine months, I guess. Still." I raised an eyebrow. "I'm taking you home and getting Makayla to take care of you. Yeah. She'd like the responsibility."

As I walked away from the crossroads with the pygmy goat bouncing at my heels, I thought I saw another flash of white in the trees. But it was probably nothing.

I called a cab back. It wasn't cheap.

La tumba del diablo. The words crept around the corners of my brain, stepped into the light of translation, but then retreated back into the darkness of half-understanding.

The Devil's Grave? Hm. I pulled out my phone and looked it up. Yep, it was a real place, not too far outside of Mexico City. "It most certainly is *not* the devil's grave." I snorted to myself. "I *know* where the devil's grave is."

"What's that?" the cab driver asked me.

I grinned too widely. "Nothing. Just an old joke. Without a punchline."

I saw the sharp disapproval cross his face that can only come from someone who regularly sees the drunkenest of humanity. He said nothing.

I didn't care.

"Laura!" I called, a little more alarmedly than I meant to as I burst in the door.

She came pounding down the stairs. "What? Is everything alright?" She looked sideways at me. "Were you out? And is that a goat?"

I glanced down at the thing. "What? Yeah. It's for Mak." I looked into her eyes. "Let's take a trip."

She put fists to her hips. "We're not going to the Pitcairn Islands."

I smiled. "No, not Pitcairn." I raised an eyebrow. "Not *yet*. How about Mexico?"

"Isn't that a bit touristy? You know how I feel about having to pay for chairs on the beach."

"Not on the beach. How about central Mexico? There's a place called *La tumba del diablo.* The Devil's Grave. How's that for nature rhyming?"

Laura took the last step down the stairs and came toward me without breaking eye contact. "That's more than a rhyme. That's the universe telling us something." Her eyes lit up and chased the remaining darkness from my side. We should go for Christmas – the anniversary of ... you know."

"The events that almost killed us?"

"The crisis that brought the family back together."

The blueness in me that came from that time was something I lived with daily. "Those events don't need commemoration."

"But wouldn't it be fun? I kind of want to dance on it." She sidled up to me, swaying to imaginary music, and took my hand. "Dance with me on the devil's grave, love? You did a good thing. It deserves to be remembered. You know, rituals are how we whisper our deeds to the higher powers who guide us."

"Hmph," I said and pulled on my beard.

She put a hand on each of my thighs and leaned into my face. "Dance with me on the devil's grave one year after you sent him to hell?" She leaned in closer and whispered in my ear. "That would be hot." She gently bit my earlobe and pulled away. "Do we have a deal?"

"Fine. Deal." *Deal*. The word just slipped out. I guess I hadn't learned yet to be a little wary about that particular four-letter word.

I smiled at her, honestly and genuinely, and watched her skip off to book flights.

"Two weeks? And over Christmas?" Mak groaned when we told her we were going away. "But my *friends*!" She cast her eyes down knowing full well she wasn't going to get far with that argument.

"But *school*," she tried again. "I seriously don't think I can be away from my homework for that long. Not now. And the goat? Who's going to feed it?"

Laura and I looked at each other, and I nodded at her to pull the trigger on this.

"Makayla, hon – you're not coming. This will be just your dad and me."

I could see her puzzling it out, just like she did when she was two with her barnyard puzzles, trying to get the right animal into the right shaped hole. And then, just like with the puzzles, I watched it all click into place.

"And – then where will I stay? Here? I think I should stay here. You need somebody to stay here. I can take in the mail and I can shovel the walk and just do all the house stuff. Yeah, yeah. I think I should probably stay here."

She would've gone on, but I didn't have the heart to let her. I turned to Laura. "What do you think, sweetie? Should we leave her here? Two weeks is a long time."

"Oh, stop it, Wood," Laura laughed. "Don't leave her on the hook."

Makayla looked expectantly at me. I held on for a few more seconds and pulled my beard in mock deliberation. "Yeah, I suppose it is a good idea to have somebody stay here. You think you're up for it, Mak? We'll be back just after Christmas. You'll have Christmas dinner with grandma and grandpa."

She nodded in mute bewilderment.

"All right. I've got two conditions. Condition one – abide by whatever conditions your mother says."

Makayla continued nodding. If she had a tail, she would have been wagging it.

"Condition two – no more cheap beer." I paused a second. "There's a case of the good stuff downstairs. Drink that instead. Laura – what would you like to add to that?"

"Oh, I can think of a few things. The first is not drinking *any* beer. Come on, let's go make a list."

As they left, I sank into the couch and noticed something metal on a side table between a Kleenex box and an empty coffee cup. It was my magic harp. The one I'd given back to Mr. Blue. And then found again. And then cast into the woods at the crossroads.

Godammit.

I didn't care anymore. I blew into it, this time with more force than I had at the crossroads, and a low, mournful, train whistle sound filled the room. Night came tumbling out of me, and my Papa Scratch-made memories dried up. It felt like I was exorcising the unholiness of that Christmas. It felt like the sun just came out. It felt like warmth or water or life itself had suddenly returned to some dried-up plot of land. It felt good.

I needed to take this harp on the trip. I wanted to blow a note of pure joy and glee over *la tumba del diablo* and slow time so I could enjoy that moment for an eternity. I wanted to puff out a merry tune as I kicked the dirt on the devil's grave and Laura danced, naked and pagan, in some kind of ancient ecstasy. I needed to take this with me.

The warmth of the little thing increased, heating my fingers past comfort. I tossed it back between Kleenex and mug. No. No, I wouldn't bring it with me. This trip was supposed to be an escape from all the supernatural stuff. Bringing this thing would surely just be inviting more of all that bad juju. No, I wanted this trip to be clean. I wanted this trip to be … what?

Holy. It was the only word I could think of that fit. Not in the churchy or do-right-to-others sense or anything like that. But clean. Pure. Holy.

And the enchanted mouth harp from an undead hound of hell that magically appeared back in my possession didn't feel particularly clean, pure or holy. No, it would stay here, forgotten on its end table until I happened to notice it again.

The flight connections were tight, but, if everything went to plan, we could be dancing on *la tumba del diablo* at the exact *minute*, one year later, that Papa Scratch had burned. We didn't spend any time in Mexico City – we caught a bus the night we landed and went to a little town a couple of hours away. San Juan del Río. The next day we'd rent a car and drive the twenty minutes or so to the devil's grave.

It was well after one in the morning, but the clerk at the Hotel Colonial was up waiting for us when we got in. From behind the desk, I heard music, but not the *banda* that I expected. This was ancient – as if it came from somewhere at the dawn of human time, all scratchy and full of ripe pain and dry suffering. It sounded familiar.

"This music – who is it?"

The clerk shrugged. *"Es musica americana."* She tossed a CD case to me and picked up our bags.

Color drained out of the brightly painted hotel courtyard and everything fell away. There, smiling at me under his trim mustache from a CD case in central Mexico, was Papa Scratch, grinning and wrapping his spider-leg fingers around a guitar. He wore the same old-fashioned, double-breasted suit I'd known him in, the same hat perched rakishly on his head.

I felt Laura's hand on my shoulder. "Wood? What's the matter, hon?"

I showed her the case. "It's him. That's Papa Scratch. That's the devil."

"What?" She took it from me and read. *"Blind Mug Walker. The complete recordings*. This is Mug Walker."

I cocked an eyebrow. "It's Papa Scratch. That's what he looked like."

She forced a smile and tried to make light of the situation. "Wood, love – you're going to have to bone up on old blues musicians and arcane incantations if you're going to go around slaying devils."

She seemed like she expected me to laugh. I didn't even look at her.

She continued, less jokey now. "They say he made a deal with the devil to get the ability to play the blues better than anyone living. But he died early. Nobody knows how." She paused. "How do you not know this story?"

The music ran down me like a chill.

194

took a deep breath, but nothing made it into my lungs, and I coughed and sputtered.

I caught a glimpse of Laura down a long colonnade being led away by the hand of someone who'd already turned the corner.

"Laura!" I thought I screamed, but the thin air in my lungs made it little more than a whisper.

I ran, my oxygen-starved legs now rebelling against me with every pace. From what I knew of this world, this was my only chance. If I lost her now, I'd just lose her.

I ran with a sickness in my stomach about what I'd find when I turned that corner. I ran against the resistance in my body and mind.

She wasn't there. Neither was whoever led her away. It was a long, narrow alley, forking at the end. Houses bedecked in brightly colored tile lined its sides. I walked slowly without destination along the little stone lane with the cobbles digging into the thin soles of my shoes.

Damn it! I was done with this. I'd had enough devil-dealing and freaky alternate planes of existence in my life. Why do they all keep bothering me? What did I ever do to any of them?

The wind blew scattered syllables down the grey lane.

Wood Sweeney, devil slayer.

I remembered the words of the old woman on the street. The words of Willie Brown. Devil slayer. Me. Was that what this was all about? Was this revenge for what I'd done to Papa Scratch? The devils and demons and hellhounds that I'd met didn't particularly seem like the loyal kind – would they seriously go to this much trouble just to punish me for offing their old boss? A sharp, hot shiver shot up the nerves of my spine as I thought of the prospect of seeing Mr. Blue, Ms. Fallen and Mr. Pale again. I kept walking. It didn't matter. Once I found Laura, all of this would be over. I'd make sure of it. I didn't know how, but I'd make sure of it.

Devil slayer.

No. I was no devil slayer. Not anymore. I was just going to find my wife and leave all of this behind me. Forever.

Devil slayer.

"Leave me alone," I said. My voice sounded small and distant.

The air became crowded with an acidic, oily smoke. I coughed and gagged and felt the inside of my lungs coated with the stuff. I retched a dry heave that only made things worse when I needed to gasp again at the greasy air.

I came to the fork in the little alley – a Y-shaped, three-way crossroads with one branch leading off into dusty underbrush and cactuses, the other, the left-hand road, into darkness. The smoke settled low to the ground and obscured my feet on the hard cobbles. It was sucked into a foot-high, rusted iron grating against the stones of the road at the point in the fork ahead of me.

I wasn't going to look in it. No way.

Devil slayer.

Aw, hell.

I crouched down and squinted into the half-light behind the grate. The pit down there was filled with the same kind of light, moon-white stones that cobbled this half-street.

I looked closer. They weren't stones.

The elongated ones tipped me off first, but when I saw the empty, hollow eyes of the skull staring back at me, I knew they weren't stones. They were human bones.

I knew I shouldn't have looked.

I felt something heavy in my pocket, something that felt like it pulled at the seams of my clothes. I fished around in my pants and pulled it out. It was my magic mouth harp.

I'd left it at home. I could picture it on the end table between the mug and the Kleenex box. I'd left it at home intentionally. And yet it was in my hand.

It was one of those times where the context, the situation itself, seems to take over the driving, and I was just in the passenger seat watching it all go by. I knew if I put my breath through the reeds of that harp, I would be a part of the devil's unholy world again.

Aw, hell.

I closed my eyes and breathed out slowly through my nose, emptying my lungs of all the oily air. Then, with my lips tight around the metal of the harp, I drew in breath, and the reeds responded with a slow, curled, mournful, sepia note that resounded against the cobbles and the iron grates and the bones tossed into the ossuary below.

Night swirled from the wound in my ribs, draining black into the ossuary. The dead bones rattled and stirred.

And I thought I heard a voice whisper *devil slayer*.

Acknowledgements

I'd always thought the act of writing was a solo endeavor. Maybe it is, but the act of getting a book out takes a village.

I'd like to thank Keeley Grier for a long discussion about police procedure (which I only took a little dramatic license with) and for schooling me about the fentanyl crisis, which brought a depth to the story that I didn't see before.

I'd like to thank Jack Harlan, the Mortician Musician, for reawakening that bluesy part of myself during a long-overdue reunion. I thought that part of me passed away with my teens. jackharlan.ca

I'd like to thank the good people at NaNoWriMo for organizing the event that gave birth to this book in the first place. They do good work. Support them. nanowrimo.org

I'd like to thank Tony Phillips for doing NaNoWriMo with me in 2016 and especially for not getting nearly as many words per day as I did. He always knows how to make me feel good about myself. amazon.com/Tony-Phillips

I'd like to thank Lacy Lieffers for her sharp proofreading of this, and for showing me around Saskatoon (where this story is secretly set – shh) while I was writing this, and for being around to share looks with during that intense talk with Dennis at Winston's pub.

Speaking of Saskatoon, I'd like to thank the *Bon Temps Café* for having some of the best gumbo and po' boys I've had at a time when I needed them most. I'd also like to thank Andres Martin del Campo, the sculptor of that fantastic piece on the back wall of *Bon Temps* that lent itself to a central scene in this book. bontempscafe.ca

I'd like to thank Darryl and our chat on a downtown Saskatoon street for serving as the inspiration for Willie Brown.

I'd like to thank all my glorious beta readers. Laurie Zottman for deepening a character I had no idea how to. Check out the blog she shares with an imaginary raccoon.

darklittlecritter.com. I'd like to thank Sarah L. Johnson and Dorian Mills for finding every single god-damned point in the book where I said *yeah, good enough* and exposing it to the harsh light of day. But also for giving more-often-than-not brilliant ways of fixing each one. Check out Sarah's writing. sarahljohnson.com

This book depended so much on music. Robert Johnson, of course, so I'd like to thank Brian Grier, my father-in-law for lending me his copy of *The Complete Recordings* (and for his beta reading). I'd also like to thank whoever put together the 2013 collection of blues songs called *Devil Got My Woman* (with the great cover showing the devil and a naked lady – nice!). Those tracks were the fuel that kept this book going. Finally, during the excruciating process of edits, it was Bob Dylan's *Street Legal*, especially that last track, that got me through editing and helped me find a grip on the bits of the story I was missing.

I'd like to thank my wife and my mother-in-law, Koré Grier and Jan Grier, for their eagle-eyed editing and support. I firmly believe a book is only as good as its worst typo, and these two women made this book great.

And, of course, I'd like to thank my father for never walking away no matter how hard it must have gotten.

About the Author

After meeting the devil herself at a lonely crossroads not far outside of Swift Current, Saskatchewan, Jim Jackson got an exclusive interview with the Princess of Darkness and a short-lived staff position as her PR writer. From that gig, he came away with a supernatural ability to tell a tale, putting him up there with liars like Herodotus, the guy who sold me all that land in Florida, and Donald Trump.

But he's modest about his talent. "What's this interview for?" he confided to me, taking a long swig of Bordeaux. "How did you get this number?" Powerful words.

An author, public speaking instructor, wine lover and amateur blues musician, Jim can be found on the lonely, sepia-hued plains of Southern Alberta, or traveling the country, notebook, corkscrew and mouth harp in hand, looking for really good stories. What's yours? Sit down. Grab a glass. Tell your story.

www.reallygoodstory.com
@jacksontron
https://www.facebook.com/Jim-Jackson-580484732146598
https://www.amazon.com/Jim-Jackson/e/B01LX5NJ6O

Advance Praise

Stones in My Passway is prose as blue note jazz. A story with equal parts whimsy and darkness, it imagines an answer to the question we all ask in midlife – what if? What if you could know how it could have been? What if you could scratch the itch of unanswered pondering? What if the art that dwelt in our young hearts lived into adult fruition?

Jim Jackson, Canada's storyteller for the 21ˢᵗ Century, weaves together timeless themes and ultra-modern realism in a story for our cynical age. The book reconceives the possibilities of print and presents a tale as soundtrack, blue notes tripping behind the beat with lyrics pushing the pace. From the angst of middle age to the promise of knowing through the mind of the Devil himself, *Stones in My Passway*, with its liner notes for life, is a most uncommon work of from a true impresario.

Tony Philips, author of *The Fires of Orc*

Papa Scratch will return in …

A NOVEL IN BLUES

#2 in the **Papa Scratch** trilogy

DEVIL
got
my WOMAN

a novel of wives, women,
and devil dealing

jim jackson

coming soon!